Death of an Atheist

P.G. Hungerland

Walking Path Press

Published by Walking Path Press

ISBN 978-1-988604-11-4
Second Edition

Cover Image from Arnold Böcklin's Self-Portrait with Death as a Fiddler (between 1871 and 1874)

ONE

THE GREAT ATHEIST was discovered under a waterfall in the Swiss Alps, face down in a pool, sunken below the surface. His arms were outstretched in a posture of crucifixion—or as if he'd leaped off the cliff in an absurd attempt to fly. The sight of him was all the more unsettling because I had prayed, the night before, for a sign from God.

After the Munich family, I was the first to see the body. It was morning and I had just left the hotel, following a footpath through the meadow toward the waterfall. The Pfannli, it was called. I'd seen it yesterday from the clifftop, and now I wanted to take a photograph from below. There had been rain overnight and the meadow was damp and the drops were still falling out of the sky, heavy and spaced far apart, hardly touching me as I walked.

The mountains about me were draped in snow and scarfs of cloud, the lower slopes blanketed with forests and meadows and dotted with chalets. A cowbell was clanging somewhere and I found myself looking up and about. The shrouded peaks made you wonder what lay beyond them: hope and expectation were built into the landscape.

A woman emerged through the trees ahead, hurrying toward me with a look of fear, pulling along a small girl with one hand and a boy with the other. I'd seen the woman and her family in the dining hall yesterday and overheard they were from Munich. Frau Munich, I'll call her. The skin on her face was thin and tight like cellophane wrapped over bone.

'Hilfe! Da ist ein toter Mann!' she cried.

I told her I didn't speak German, and she reverted to English, glancing back toward the trees: 'There is a man under the waterfall! I think he is dead!'

She didn't wait for my response and hurried on, bobbing to and fro as she dragged the children toward the hotel. I ran through the trees and saw Frau Munich's husband wading into the waterfall pool.

He was up to his knees and glanced at me as I approached, but said nothing. The body was visible beneath the rippling surface. Arms outstretched. Embracing death.

Herr Munich took one of the legs and pulled it toward him. The body drifted closer and the German caught hold of an arm, a checkered shirt sleeve. The limb bent freely; I realized that rigor mortis had not yet set in.

I'd learned about rigor mortis when my father died.

Herr Munich was lean and strong, his arms wrapped in veins, and he grasped the floating figure with both hands and flipped it around easily. As the corpse turned I beheld the face of an old man, his gaze frozen and narrowed, peering up through the clear water. Even in death there was a glow of wisdom in his expression, in the pensive wrinkles and the hawk-wing brows and the affable old bags under his eyes. It was Sir Kenneth Chatwin. There was a red crack in his head where the ear should have been.

I felt sick and looked away. Herr Munich dragged the body to the edge of the pool.

'Er muss gefallen sein,' he said, gazing up at the cliff.

'Yes,' I said, understanding. 'He fell.'

The cliff was about forty metres high. Near the bottom was a bulge of rock. Most of the falling water skirted past this bulge but some of the stream deflected off it, spattering droplets over us. Sir Kenneth's head must have slammed into it.

Another bolt of sickness went through me. I remembered my prayer from last night: *Lord, my faith is weak. Help me to believe in you. Give me a sign that you are real.*

If this, a fresh corpse, was God's answer to my prayer, then it was a cruel one.

It had to be a coincidence.

We stared at him. The ripples lapped at his shoes. He was gone, quite gone, like an actor pulled suddenly off the stage, leaving behind his mask and costume in a useless heap. The moment demanded nothing but our horrified attention.

It was a relief to hear voices drifting toward us. My friend, Jeremy Flange, was the first to come dashing through the trees, followed by Leo Granger and Sir Kenneth's students, Delia Stoltz and Zach Blakey. They had flown in to Switzerland over the past few days and had gathered this morning in the hotel café to discuss the conference. Sir Kenneth had been expected at that meeting. They must have heard Frau Munich's shouting as she came in the doors.

Their voices dwindled as they beheld the scene. Herr Munich, who had stepped back into the water, picked out a hiking pole and laid it next to Sir Kenneth, whose narrow gaze was fixed on the bleak sky as if he had spotted something curious, as if he was not lying there with a gaping crack in his head.

Flange glanced at me with quiet shock. Delia Stoltz gave a cry and ran off through the trees. Zach Blakey stumbled backwards and began retching into a bush, and at the same moment the hotel manager ran up. He was a short man in a pink dress shirt. He halted before the body, clutching his face, panting with agitation.

'Mein Gott! Mein Gott!'

The waterfall clattered indifferently. A slug, plump and brown, the size of a cigar, was creeping over the ground toward the dead man's fingers. Leo Granger swept the intruder away with the tip of his sandal and then pulled out a handkerchief, leaned over the body, and draped it on the face. I thought about my prayer again. *Give me a sign...*

A coincidence. It had to be.

TWO

THERE WERE FOUR policemen in the village and they arrived together in sporty blue jackets. They examined the corpse and then briefly questioned Herr Munich and the rest of us while the dead man waited at the edge of the pool, shoes wavering in the ripples.

'We ask that you remain in the hotel until the detective comes,' one of the officers told us.

'The detective?' Granger said. 'Why did you call a detective?'

'He will have more questions.'

'But there's no crime here. It's obvious what happened, isn't it? He slipped off the cliff.'

'It rained overnight,' Flange added. 'The ground was slick this morning.'

'A man is dead,' the officer said with undeterred seriousness. 'We must investigate.'

The paramedics arrived on the scene just then, although their haste dissolved once they laid eyes on Sir

Kenneth. After a brief examination they placed him on a stretcher, covered him with a grey blanket, and carried him away. The rest of us followed in a grim procession through the trees and across the meadow.

The hotel was perched on a grassy slope nearby, puffing wisps of smoke through a tin chimney. The Iselin, the place was called. It had three wings, all built of timber, like a trio of oversized chalets that faced the valley at various angles, capturing the best mountain views. It was late June, just before the summer season, and there were few guests. Most would be arriving later today and tomorrow for the conference.

We walked around the building and stood on the porch, watching as the paramedics lifted the body into the back of the van.

'I can't believe he's dead,' Flange said. 'And *here*, of all places.'

'What do you mean?'

'The world's greatest atheist has died within a stone's throw of a Christian establishment.'

He was referring to the Iselin itself. It was, like certain other hotels in Switzerland, a 'Christian' hotel. Although not clearly advertised as such, there were signs of it here and there, like the religious magazines in the lobby, or the scenic cards with Bible verses awaiting each new guest, upon each fluffy pillow, along with a piece of wrapped chocolate.

It was, as everyone knows, an irony that a conference on atheism should be held at the Iselin. Flange had already told me how it happened: Sir Kenneth and his wife, Eleanor, spent a month each summer in Switzerland. Eleanor had enjoyed many vacations in the country during her childhood, and her older sister, Margaret, later moved here and bought a chalet in the village. When Sir Kenneth came up with the idea of holding a 'humanist' conference in Switzerland, Eleanor mentioned it to Margaret, and Margaret—who had heard fine things about the Iselin—was quick to recommend the place. But Margaret didn't realize that the Iselin was a religious establishment, and the German-speaking staff at the hotel who booked the conference didn't realize that 'humanist' meant 'atheist'. So it was, by a stroke of mutual misunderstanding, that the atheists and the Iselin were brought together.

Of course, some people would later suggest that the staff of the Iselin were well aware of the true nature of the conference from the beginning and had deliberately overlooked the booking 'error' as a means of luring two hundred atheists into a Christian lion's den. In any case, it was too late to do anything about the error once it was realized; money had been transferred, conference materials printed. Newspapers also soon picked up the story, which turned out to be good fortune for the atheists, who would never have gotten so much attention.

'Needless to say, it's a coincidence,' Flange continued. 'He could have died anywhere. But there will probably be conspiracy theories. Atheists will think a religious fanatic pushed him off the cliff. Then again, people who believe in God will probably think that God pushed him off the cliff. Divine justice and all that.' The ambulance drove off. Flange looked at me. 'I assume that's not what *you* think?'

'What, that God killed him?' I said with a faint laugh. 'I'm just an Anglican, Flange. What would I know about God's will?'

*

We went back inside and I waited in my room. It was on the first floor, with a balcony facing the meadow. I could see the policemen wandering about the clifftop where the waterfall came down in a thin stream, vanishing behind the pine trees below.

Despite the tragedy of the morning, the peace and beauty of the valley remained unshaken. On the near horizon was a great mountain, broad-shouldered and snowy, like a king in a white mantle presiding over the village. A little closer was a summit known as the Alpkäppli. A magnificent waterfall spilled off its grassy alp, tumbling down a long rocky slope in a slender mass of white tresses. It was a larger, grander version of the little falls from which Sir Kenneth had slipped.

Assuming he slipped.

There was a knock at the door. It was the detective. He introduced himself as Inspector Schwartzentaub. The name, I understand, may be translated as 'Black Dove'—or 'Black Deaf'. I prefer the former, since his balding head was, in fact, round as a dove's, with a sheen that gleamed in the pot lights.

We shook hands. 'Conner Bachman,' I said.

'Bachman? Are you a Swiss?'

'One half of me was, two hundred years ago. My father's side of the family came from this part of the country. My mother's half is Irish.'

'Ah, Irish,' he said with polite disappointment. We sat by the window and he began his interview. 'Did you know Mr Kenneth Chatwin?' he said.

'Sir Kenneth,' I said. 'I was introduced to him yesterday over supper. That was the first and only time I spoke with him. I didn't see him again until this morning at the waterfall. After he had died.' I told him everything that had happened from when I had left the hotel that morning until the paramedics arrived.

Black Dove jotted notes on a pad. 'Do you know why Sir Kenneth went up to the cliff today?'

'Apparently he'd been going up there every morning since he arrived last Tuesday. The hotel manager mentioned it. It was Sir Kenneth's habit. An early morning walk. I understand he went up using the steps in the cliff wall.' I gestured out the window toward the cliff. Black Dove leaned over, peering out. The steps were ingeniously fashioned out of the natural contours of the rock, with a rope railing along the jagged wall. 'It's an easy climb,' I said. 'I went up yesterday afternoon. It takes two or three minutes. Sir Kenneth had a slight limp, so he might have gone up more slowly.'

'He limped?'

'He suffered a stroke last summer.'

'A what?' Black Dove said quizzically. His English was decent but imperfect.

I tapped the side of my head. 'Bleeding in the left side of his brain. He had a remarkable recovery, they say. Except for the limp. It was on the right side.'

'The stroke was on the left side, but the limp was on the right?'

'The connections in the brain are crossed. Left controls right and vice versa.'

'You are a doctor?'

'No. But I have a background in neuropsychology. I'm doing a PhD.'

'I see. Now tell me, Mr Bachman, when did you arrive in the village?'

'I arrived yesterday afternoon around one o'clock. I flew in to Zurich on Friday, from Toronto, and stayed until Sunday to do some sightseeing. Then I took the train to Frutigen via Spiez, and then the bus to the village.'

'And you met Sir Kenneth at supper last evening?'

'That's correct. Jeremy Flange introduced us. Mr Flange works with Professor Granger. They're all from the same university. Zach Blakey, one of Sir Kenneth's graduate students, was there as well. We sat at the same table, but apart from the introduction I didn't speak with Sir Kenneth. He was seated at the other end.'

'Do you recall anything about him?'

'He looked tired. He was quieter than I would have expected. I've read his books and seen videos of his talks.

I thought he would be more energetic. Mind you, he did become quite upset at one point. I'm not sure if it's relevant.'

'Yes?'

'It was just for a few moments before supper. The waitress was saying grace for some people at another table. Two elderly couples.'

'What do you mean by *grace*?'

'She was praying before the meal. She was speaking in German but it was obviously a prayer. Their eyes were closed.' I remembered her with a pinch of desire: she was pretty as a milk maid, with blond hair that was neatly tied up, showing the back of her neck. 'Most of the group at our table seemed uncomfortable with the prayer,' I said.

'Uncomfortable?'

'They're atheists, so it's expected. But then, when the prayer was finished, Professor Granger muttered something about them being "so primitive"—the people who'd prayed. That's when Sir Kenneth snapped. He said, "Dammit, don't be so bloody arrogant!" He said it in a low voice, but he was furious. It took everyone by surprise.'

'Did he continue to be angry afterward?'

'It was just for that moment. He was quiet then. We were all quiet for a bit.'

'Do you know where he went after supper?'

'He and Professor Granger went out to the hotel porch.'

'Just the two of them?'

'Yes, they were talking. I saw them as I stepped out that evening with Mr Flange. I didn't see Sir Kenneth again until this morning.'

'Where did you and Mr Flange go?'

'To the village for a drink. We returned to the Iselin around eight thirty or nine. It had started to rain then. Professor Granger had also been out and he arrived at the same time we did.'

'He was on his own?'

'Yes.'

'And then what happened?'

'Then I went to my room.'

'And you remained there.'

'No, I came out a few minutes later to get a cup of tea from the hotel café.'

'And that was all?'

'I saw Mr Flange and Professor Granger at the billiards table. There's a table just off the corridor. You would have passed it on the way here. Mr Blakey was with them too. Mr Flange invited me to join in the game but I declined and returned to my room. I slept through the night, and this morning I woke around seven thirty and went for breakfast. Everybody was there but Sir Kenneth.'

'Who is everybody?'

'The same people who were at supper yesterday. Mr Flange, Professor Granger, and Mr Blakey. We all sat at the same table. Delia Stoltz was there as well—for breakfast, I mean. She wasn't at supper last night. She's another one of Sir Kenneth's students.'

'Where was she?'

'I have no idea.'

'How do you know these people?'

'I only know Mr Flange. Mr Flange and I are old friends.'

'Was Sir Kenneth's wife at breakfast as well?'

'No. I haven't seen her at all. I didn't know she was in the village.'

'So last night was the first and the last time you saw Sir Kenneth?'

'Yes.'

Black Dove nodded, flipping his notebook shut. 'You are an atheist like the others, Mr Bachman? That is why you have come here?'

'Actually, I'm Anglican.'

'Oh? You believe in God?'

'Yes. I'm giving a talk on religion and moral behaviour. Mr Flange invited me.'

'You said he was an old friend?'

'We attended the same church as teenagers. He became an atheist in university whereas I continued along the straight and narrow, so to speak. We got in touch again last year, and when he heard about my research he invited me to the conference.'

'How interesting. Does he wish to unconvert you, perhaps?' Black Dove said with a faint smile.

'You'll have to ask Mr Flange that. As far as I can see we respect each other's views. And we're both students of the mind, which gives us something in common.'

'Of course.' Black Dove placed his card on the table. 'Thank you, Mr Bachman. You may call me at this number if you have any other information that might help us.'

THREE

DURING THE COURSE of the interview fresh clouds had begun spilling into the valley as if a dam of fog had broken somewhere. The rain thickened to a steady downpour that became heaviest at noon, just as the first conference guests arrived.

Among them was a group of six student volunteers from Oxford, the members of a humanist association. Sir Kenneth had been involved with the group since his undergraduate days and had invited them to assist with the proceedings.

I was on my way to the dining hall when they came in; I saw Flange greeting them and breaking the news. The students looked stunned in their dripping jackets and backpacks.

'I just can't believe it,' said a young man with a damp scruff of hair. His girlfriend, a snub-nosed creature with red cheeks, leaned against his shoulder and began sobbing. She wore a button that read *Keep Your Rosaries*

Off My Ovaries.

I hesitated at the corner of the reception desk, feigning interest in a newspaper. 'I realize this is difficult and unexpected,' Flange said. 'But I can tell you that Sir Kenneth had been very much looking forward to your coming here. He was always nostalgic about his Oxford days.'

'But is the conference still going ahead?' sniffled the Ovaries woman.

'Absolutely,' Flange replied with reassuring cheerfulness. 'It's going forward as planned. It's how he would have wanted it. Keep fighting the good fight! That's what Ken always said.'

Fighting the good fight: an old Christian expression. I might have laughed at the irony, except that the young atheists looked serious, nodding bravely.

I slipped away to the dining hall. The tables were mostly empty. The two elderly couples had checked out that morning. The Munich family was seated at one end of the hall and Leo Granger and Zach Blakey at the other end. I noticed that the cutlery and dishware had been removed from Sir Kenneth's place.

Blakey mumbled hello. There was a greenish dab on his chin, a bit of leek and potato soup, not far from two brownish moles, creating a quaint triangle. I took my seat and the milk-maid waitress arrived with my bowl. The rim was wide and sprinkled with herb-like bits of blue and yellow and violet.

'What are these?' I said.

'Dried wildflowers,' she said. 'From the mountains. I am sorry that you have lost your friend.'

She granted me a kind smile and departed. Granger spooned his soup in brooding silence. He had a scraggly beard that sprouted from his cheeks in coarse brown and grey threads. Blakey and I kept our conversation quiet and didn't talk about Sir Kenneth or the police until Flange arrived a few minutes later. 'The news is already out,' he said, showing us his phone.

The headline was *Sir Kenneth Chatwin Falls to Death in Alps*. Below was a picture of him, a black-and-white photo, the usual one from his books: a wise-looking man with hands folded under his chin, regarding the viewer with an expression of charm and wonder.

We compared our interviews with Inspector Black Dove. 'He made me feel like a criminal with all his questions,' Flange said.

'It's just a routine investigation,' Granger muttered. 'They have to go through the motions.'

'But there's nothing to investigate. Anybody can see that it was an accident. We should have warned him not to go up there. And climbing up in that fog? With that limp?'

'I didn't notice any fog this morning,' I said.

'It was quite thick around six.'

'I didn't realize you were such an early riser.'

'I'm still jet-lagged. I was just dozing off when I heard a baby crying. That's when I looked out the window and couldn't see a thing.'

'I heard the crying too,' Blakey said.

'Are you sure it was a baby?' I said.

They agreed that it was; and they agreed it seemed to be coming from outside, from somewhere in the meadow.

'What difference does it make?' Granger said.

'None,' Flange said. 'None at all. But it must have been around the time he died. The woman at the front desk mentioned that he left the hotel at a quarter to six. Poor Eleanor, she must be devastated. The police took her to Frutigen to identify the body.'

'Has she been at the hotel all this time?' I said.

'She's staying with her sister in the village,' Blakey said.

'Enough,' Granger said irritably. 'This isn't a talk show.' He glanced over his shoulder. 'Where the hell's the food?'

I noticed the Munich boy eyeing us from behind a pillar. He was five or six years old, with a loose front tooth dangling from a bit of flesh like a crude ornament.

'I almost forgot,' Flange said. 'The volunteers from Oxford have arrived. I gave them a hundred francs from the conference fund. They're going to set up a memorial in the lobby. I thought it was a good idea. There'll be a display board with photos, a table with Ken's books, a donation box for charity.'

'That should keep them busy,' Granger said.

'Have you thought about the opening address for the conference?'

'Not yet. We'll have to figure something out.'

'I understand that Ken was going to talk about the state of atheism. The future direction of the movement. I suppose we might want to shift the focus onto Ken himself at this point? His life. His accomplishments.'

Granger sighed wearily. 'You're probably right. Blakey, can you pull some pictures off the website? Pictures of Ken getting awards, that sort of thing.'

'I'll see what we have. I'll look on the Internet.'

Flange began tapping hastily on his phone. 'And I'm sending you a couple right now—these are from a few days ago. They should be on your phone in a second.' He turned toward the window. 'Now let's pray the weather brightens—pray in the secular sense, of course. It might help lift the mood.'

I looked outside. The window faced the Grüneggli ridge on the eastern side of the valley. It was a craggy, snow-spotted mountain laced with streams. The rain had softened but the clouds were still heavy and floating ponderously, catching against the lower wooded slopes.

'I hope I'm not interrupting.'

It was one of the volunteers, the young man with the damp scruff of hair. It was still damp and scruffy, apparently a kind of fashion. He looked like a lama after a shower.

'Ah, Malcolm,' Flange said. 'We were just talking about the memorial. This is Professor Leo Granger, who I'm sure you've heard of, and this is my friend Conner and my colleague Zach. Is everything in order?'

'A pleasure to meet you all. Yes, I've sent Leanne and Christopher to fetch some things from the village. However, I've received an email, a somewhat troubling message. It's from the American contingent.'

'The who?' Granger said.

'The volunteers from America. The Princeton group. They're heading over on the train at the moment, and it seems they've encountered a group of Christian fundamentalists who claim to be coming to the conference.'

'Christian fundamentalists?' Flange said.

'Our friends estimated thirty of them. Now that was the estimate for the train. According to another message—we're getting various messages, you see—it appears that fundies from several countries are heading this way. A lot of Germans and British. They've booked hotel rooms and rentals in the village. They're going to set up an anti-conference.'

'An anti-conference?' Granger said. 'What is an anti-conference?'

'I assume they intend to counter our own proceedings.'

Granger looked at me. 'Are you involved in this?'

'Me?'

'Aren't you Catholic?'

'I'm Anglican.'

'Oh, don't worry about Conner Bachman,' Flange said with a harmless laugh. 'He's no fundamentalist. In fact, his faith is hanging by a thread. Why else do you think he's here?'

FOUR

I DIDN'T PLAN on telling people I believed in God, although I knew that Flange might mention it to Granger and that word could get around. So I was ready to be confronted at some point—to be accused of being irrational or unscientific. But I didn't expect to be accused of plotting against the conference itself. I might have said something to Granger in my own defence, had the milk maid not arrived just then with plates of veal and rösti.

The sight of meat and potatoes restored a sense of reason. Zach Blakey pointed out that hateful messages often showed up on Sir Kenneth's website, and the frequency of the ravings had only increased since the conference was announced last year. It was hardly surprising that a few fanatical groups had concocted a plan to disrupt the event.

At this, Granger appeared satisfied and retreated gloomily into his meal, while Flange, Blakey and I moved on to the neutral subject of scholarship funding. We were finishing dessert when Delia Stoltz arrived in a mood as sullen as Granger's. The police had only just gotten around to her, she said. Flange probed for details but she wasn't interested in talking.

I returned to my room and lay down, worn out by the morning. I was still wounded by Granger's insinuation that I was a 'fundamentalist', although I was even more wounded by Flange's suggestion that my faith was weak—if only because that was closer to the truth.

I wondered if I ought to pray about it, although I was still troubled by my prayer from the night before. I ended up dozing off, only to be woken two hours later by Flange himself, rapping at my door. The weather had cleared, just as he'd hoped, and he wondered if I might join him for a walk in the village.

I drew the curtains and beheld the transformation. The heavy clouds had dissolved and the sun was making its first appearance since my arrival yesterday, dappling the green slopes and gleaming against the snowy mountains. The mighty waterfall that spilled off the Alpkäppli was thicker, engorged with the fresh rain of the morning.

It was a five-minute walk to the centre of the village. We didn't speak a word about Sir Kenneth's death; we both seemed to be avoiding it, at least for the moment. The main road was lined with shops and restaurants and hotels, and gondolas were traversing the slopes to our right.

'Leo was in town,' Flange said at last, returning to the unhappy matter. 'He picked up Eleanor from the police station. They're saying it was an accident. The autopsy isn't done yet, but that's what they think, off the record. It's possible he had another stroke. That might be why he fell. His body is being flown back to England in a few days. The funeral is next Sunday in Oxford.'

'Will you be going?'

'Everybody in the lab is going.'

'It's hard to believe he's dead. Such a brilliant mind.'

'Ah, but he was more than that, Conner. He was big-hearted. Great-hearted! Do you know he gave away thirty percent of his income to charity? It isn't widely known because he didn't want to make a big deal of it. But that was Ken. That's what makes him so different from other atheists. He could win debates on the facts, but that's not why people were drawn to him. They were drawn to him because he was good.'

We paused at a tennis court. Men in white shirts were slicing a ball back and forth.

'Character matters,' I said. 'Often more than intellect.'

'Both matter,' Flange said. 'And Ken had both in abundance.'

We followed a paved single-lane road up the slope. 'Years ago,' Flange went on, 'I was attracted to Jesus because he was good. He healed people and cared for children and the weak. And because he was so good, I wanted to believe that he was, in fact, who he claimed to be—the Son of God. I wanted to believe what he said about himself because I admired his character. But after a while I began to see my mistake. I realized that no matter how much I admired the man, it was the truth that mattered. Was he really the Son of God? Did he really perform miracles? Is there any evidence of God—testable, reliable evidence—or isn't there? Because if there is no evidence, it doesn't matter how much you want to believe.'

'Do you feel any spiritual instinct anymore?'

'An instinct? I think most of us feel an instinct. It's wired into our biology—a sense of hope in the face of life's trials. Even a hope we might survive death. I can still recall the days when I believed in the resurrection of the dead. Those were innocent times, Conner. Happy times. But a happy feeling doesn't justify a false idea. The dead will not be resurrected. The dead will remain were they are, fading into the dust. I wish it were otherwise, I really do. Maybe one day it will be? Maybe one day we'll find a way to revive the dead, or else to prolong life. There is wonderful work being done in the area of human enhancement. I'm talking about computer chips in the brain, hardware in the body, nanotechnology in the bloodstream. It's no longer science fiction. It's happening. Religion is an old-fashioned social technology that promises much but delivers little. The real technology has only just begun. Forgive me for preaching.'

'I'm not offended, Flange. Your optimism is infectious—even if misguided.'

He gave me a dubious glance, then smiled. The quiet lane led us into a neighbourhood of chalets. They had wide balconies with carved panels and window boxes overflowing with geraniums. The newer homes were built of a lighter timber, while the older were of a darker wood, their beams inscribed with verses in white Gothic letters.

'By the way,' Flange said. 'I'm sorry about my comment in the dining hall.'

'What comment?'

'That bit about your faith hanging by a thread.'

'You were coming to my defence. I appreciate it.'

'But is there any truth in it? I mean, do you have doubts?'

'About God?'

'Yes.'

'I suppose I have a few. I might have had more, except that my faith has never been a complicated matter. It's a rather simple faith, actually.'

'How simple?'

'Like a small boat on the big ocean of life.'

'A boat named *Jesus*, I suppose?'

'Yes. And the boat has proven sturdy and reliable. It's steered me well so far.'

'Do you ever feel tempted to jump to another boat? For example, our boat.'

'To become an atheist? No. Anyhow, becoming an atheist wouldn't be like jumping to another boat. It would be like jumping into the ocean.'

Flange clapped me on the shoulder, laughing.

'Is that why you invited me to the conference?' I said. 'To tempt me?'

'No. But if I could help you see the light, then why not?'

'I respect atheists, but I could never be one. For various reasons.'

'Such as?'

'I'm not logical enough.'

'You're very logical, Conner. You were one of the brightest people I knew growing up. It's a wonder that your faith survived university.'

'It almost didn't. My professors were fiercely anti-religious. It rubs off on you.'

A hawk was cruising overhead, eyeing the grassy slopes above the chalets. 'May I ask you a question?' Flange said. 'About your father.'

I looked at him. 'Odd that you should bring him up.'

'Why?'

'The sight of Sir Kenneth this morning reminded me of my father. Not that their situations had much in common—except the shock of someone I'd seen alive a day or two earlier, turning up dead. Nothing quite prepares a person for that.' Flange murmured in agreement. We rounded a corner and started down toward the main part of the village. 'What did you want to ask?' I said.

'I recall you becoming more religious after your father died. You were at church more often. You began reading books about God and talking about your faith more. I wonder if you turned to God as a way of coping with grief?'

'I suppose I did. It's the natural thing to do, if you believe in God.'

'Do you think you used God then—and maybe even now—as a psychological crutch?'

'We all have some sort of crutch, don't we?'

'But some crutches are more believable than others. Some crutches are more rational.'

'I agree. And I find it more rational to believe that we were created by God and exist for a purpose, whereas you find it more rational to believe that we exist because of chance and have no purpose.'

'That's not quite my position. I do believe we exist because of chance, but I never said we didn't have a purpose.'

'You can't have it both ways, Flange. If something occurs because of a random process it can't have occurred for a purpose.'

'But it may *serve* a purpose.'

'Yes, but only by accident.'

Just as I feared we might plunge into a hopeless debate, he caught me by the arm. 'Look,' he said. 'It's Eleanor.'

FIVE

SIR KENNETH'S WIFE was walking slowly toward us, a hand pressed against her brow, a small purse dangling aimlessly from her elbow.

'Ms Chatwin?' Flange said, hurrying toward her.

Eleanor was well into middle age, but must have been savagely pretty in her youth. Her eyes were feline and her lips well-formed; her hair was short, darkly dyed, and fur-like; she wore earrings and her nails were painted; yet her lingering beauty, such as it was, was utterly spoiled by grief.

'I'm so sorry,' Flange said. 'We're all heartbroken.'

'I'm afraid I'm not feeling well, Jeremy.'

'Can I help you?'

'I need to get home. To my sister's house.'

'Let me help,' he said, taking her arm.

We turned back, moving slowly up the incline. She led us around a corner to a two-story chalet; it had a chime with bright streamers over the door.

The air smelled of broth as we entered. Flange walked her into a sitting room off the main hallway, where Eleanor settled onto a burgundy couch with a high back of polished carved wood. Above it was a print I'd seen in a book on Swiss art; a painting by Albert Anker—a well-known profile of a demure farm girl peeling potatoes.

'I told you that you mustn't go out!' said a woman bursting into the room. She was older than Eleanor, with a stout face and a red nose like a turnip. 'What were you thinking? It won't do you any good to go back there! Who are these young men?'

She began speaking to us in Swiss German. 'We're from the conference,' Flange interrupted. 'I worked with Sir Kenneth. My name is Jeremy Flange and this is my friend Conner.'

'They helped me,' Eleanor said. She lay back on the couch, pressing a hand on her face. 'I'm not feeling well. I've got such a headache. Jeremy, this is my sister Margaret. Will you bring me something, Maggie? My head is killing me.'

'What did I tell her?' Margaret muttered as she went off. 'It would only make her feel worse!'

'Is there anything we can do for you?' Flange said.

'He's dead, Jeremy. My Kenneth is dead.'

'We're all in shock. Every one of us.'

'I went back there. I needed to see the place. I don't understand. He went for a walk and fell. I just don't understand. He was so careful when he walked.'

Margaret returned with a wet cloth, pills, and a glass

of water. Eleanor leaned up and took the tablets. She lay back and her sister draped the cloth carefully on her brow. Eleanor looked at me. 'I don't seem to recognize you. Were you his student?'

'No, but I am familiar with his work. He will be missed by many people.'

'Yes. Everybody admired him. Everybody.'

'We should let you rest,' Flange said.

'Please stay a moment. There was something I wanted to speak to you about. Maggie, will you excuse us? Perhaps you can offer this young man—I'm sorry, I forget your name.'

'Conner.'

'Perhaps you can offer Conner a drink.'

'But you must get your rest,' Margaret said. 'There's no use going over things.'

'Please, Maggie. I need a few minutes.'

'Suit yourself.' She turned to me: 'Come along, young man. There's tea in the kitchen. Where are you from?'

'Canada.'

'Ah, a colonial. How nice.'

Stew was bubbling on the stove. I sat at a heavy wooden table on a pew-like bench. On the wall was a display of silver spoons bearing English coats of arms.

'Goodness knows the stress that she's under,' Margaret said, filling our cups at the counter. 'It's not easy losing a husband. Not that I know much about husbands. I was married once, and only for a little while. He worked in money, my Freddie. That's what he liked to say—"I work in money"—because it made you imagine him swimming in a bathtub of the stuff. And he *was*. Ha-ha! But you mustn't think he was a bad man. He wasn't bad at all. Some might say he was quite a catch. My mistake wasn't that I fell for him, but that I fell for him for too long. If my love had only lasted a few days or weeks it might have been harmless. But to be in love for more than six months is a dangerous thing. You're liable to get married, which is very likely to end in divorce, or disappointment, or deception, or debt, or disease, or some other dreadful d-word. Death—there's another one. The worst.' She placed a tea cup before me and pointed her hairy chin toward the sitting room. 'Do you think Eleanor and Kenneth were happy? Far from it!'

'Every marriage has its challenges.'

'Are you married?'

'No.'

'A good thing,' she smiled. Her teeth were square and spaced apart like the upper wall of a medieval fort. 'After a year with Freddie I could see it wasn't going to work out. I am honest with myself, more honest than most. I told myself, "End it now, Maggie, before one year turns into a decade and you get used to being miserable. Better that you get used to being alone than to being miserable." That was the best advice I ever gave myself! Get used to being alone! Get used to cats on the window sill and friendships and bridge games and weeding the garden. Because for the most part, you see, life is not about episodes of love or other moments of great feeling, but about the duller times in-between. The duller times are what occupy the vast majority of our existence.'

'Have you gotten used to it?'

'Oh, it takes some effort, but I am not unhappy. I moved here in 1986 and I've never looked back. We came to Switzerland every summer when we were children, Eleanor and I. It's a beautiful country where everything works as it should and everybody tries to keep it that way. The Swiss are as industrious as Germans, but more exacting and tidy, and not nearly as cold. Some of them are even friendly. Life is very good here, yes. I enjoy my chalet and my vegetable garden.' She glanced toward the back door. The garden was visible through the glass. A small plot of earth with leafy plants growing in furrows.

'Has Ms Chatwin been staying with you, then? I haven't seen her at the hotel.'

Margaret slurped her tea. 'Yes, she's staying here. She'll need time to recover. Poor girl. She didn't deserve this.'

I nodded. 'It's a tragedy.'

'I love my sister very much,' she said, lowering her voice. 'Let there be no doubt about that. I wish I had warned her all those years ago not to bind herself to a man. Of course she wouldn't have listened. Love is delusional. No one ever believes it can go sour. She certainly didn't.'

'You mean it was bad in the end.'

'That is *exactly* what I mean.' She sighed, glancing toward the sitting room. 'They got into an awful row a few days ago.' She took another slurp of tea. 'I don't mean to blather.'

'I understand. But I can see that it's been painful for you, knowing that you could have predicted it from the very start.'

'Precisely! You understand me, dear boy! It's just as I said, divorce or disappointment or some other d-word. She shows up here Friday evening with her luggage and says, "I'm finished with him." And I ask her, "What is it, Eleanor, what's happened now?" She was weeping, poor creature. Refused to explain herself. She was upset for the next two days. Barely ate. I'd find her pottering about in the middle of the night muttering to herself. Then at times she'd pretend everything was fine, and get suddenly cheery, and put on some makeup, only to fall into another lurch. That was how she was as a girl. Always tried to hide her pain, and always failed. Why do you think she gets migraines like this? Pent-up suffering!'

'And she never explained what was wrong?'

'Marriage is the disease, my boy! But people want to stay blind. Blind and deluded. She'd called me from Canada to complain about him. He wasn't paying attention to her. He was distant. Then she called me from Budapest, of all places!'

'Budapest?'

'She'd gone along with him to some conference. It was just a few months ago, after he'd gotten back on his feet. He'd promised to spend time with her, but left her quite alone. Abandoned her so that he could talk to his colleagues about his philosophy of atheism or humanism—who knows what the difference is? And who cares? You can think whatever you want about whether God does or doesn't exist, and the lettuce will still grow if you water it. Anyway, what was I to tell her? What point was there in telling her the truth now? The truth is that you can't put two people together for forty-some years, like a cog and wheel, and hope the machine will run forever. Sooner or later you get a chink in the system, and it starts to grind, and things only get worse from there. And now he's dead. He was a burden in life, and he's become a burden in death. I told her not to go back there today!'

'To the cliff, you mean?'

'As if she could find solace in the place where he took his final breath.'

Flange entered the kitchen. I glimpsed Eleanor through the open door. She was on the couch with her eyes closed, a blanket pulled up to her chin.

'We should be going,' he said.

SIX

'WHAT DID SHE want to talk to you about?' I said once we were outside.

'It was a peculiar conversation,' Flange said. 'She wanted to know about Ken's mental state. Whether he was in his right mind when he died. Whether he was depressed, or said anything out of the ordinary.'

'Wouldn't she be able to tell these things better than you?'

'I guess she wanted a second opinion.'

'What did you tell her?'

'He seemed the same person to me—the same more or less. He might have been moodier than in the past, but I would chalk that up to the frustration of everything he had gone through. The stroke put him behind on all his projects and he was working hard to catch up. I wouldn't call that depression.'

'What about his mental abilities? His intelligence?'

'He wasn't one hundred percent, but close. There

were still moments when he couldn't find his words. The stroke had affected his speech. Otherwise he seemed fine. I certainly didn't see any sign of the staring spells that used to come over him.'

'Staring spells? You mean seizures?'

'The doctors weren't sure. He'd zone out without realizing it. I witnessed it a few times while visiting him in hospital. The spells were more frequent in the first months after the stroke, and I hadn't seen any since last year.'

'Why did it matter to her, his mental state?'

'Frankly, I think she was wondering if it was suicide. She never came out and said it, but she did ask several times about him being depressed.'

'Suicide seems unlikely, don't you think?'

'Quite unlikely, as far as I can see. He didn't have any reason to end his life. He was recovering well. He was moving forward in his work.'

We reached the gondola station, where I paused. 'Margaret told me a few things,' I said.

'What things?'

'That Sir Kenneth and Eleanor had fought last week. That's why Eleanor came to stay with her. That's why she left the hotel. She was upset with him—very upset. Eleanor had been unhappier lately in the marriage. Did you know that?'

'I suppose these things happen. Married couples argue. What else did Margaret tell you?'

'That she was opposed to marriage. And thought love

was delusional.'

'Well, I agree with her on that point. Love, to me, is the only thing more delusional than God.'

'Unless God *is* love, in which case you'd find them equally insane.'

'Touché,' he smiled.

We parted ways then. Flange had to get back to the Iselin, while I decided to stay out and explore a bit more.

I entered the gondola station, where a trio of vacant cars was waiting. I climbed into one and soon a buzzer sounded and the doors slammed shut. With an unsettling jolt, the gondola pulled out and rose, gliding over the tops of the pine trees. The car trembled and shook as it passed the first support tower from which the cables hung, and then it dipped and went up silently again.

The trees below were tall and Christmas-like, loaded with pinecones. Men were pitching grass on a sunny clearing not far from a cluster of wooden avalanche barriers. I noticed a path that ran through a meadow and along the cliff to the Pfannli waterfall; just beyond was the south wing of the Hotel Iselin, with its sloped roof and three rows of balconies. Way off, at the far end of the valley, I picked out a paraglider coasting in the blue.

It was cooler when I exited the gondola at the top of the mountain. It was among the lowest peaks in the village yet gave a satisfying view. Across the valley to the east, the woods clung to the middle slopes of the mountains like dark green beards, and thin strips of cloud were stretched across the higher peaks, where the snow mantles shone as if they'd been polished. The great waterfall flowing off the Alpkäppli was a lush cascade. The whole scene was spectacular yet somehow quaint, as if designed especially for tourists.

The postcard must have been invented here.

A dirt path led me along the ridge of the mountain. I wandered across a hill of grass and purple wildflowers, and found a sedimentary wall of rock that was soft as old pages; it crumbled as I brushed my fingers across it. The scent of a wood fire was wafting up from somewhere, along with the faint clanging of a cow or goat bell. I reached the crest of the hill and saw empty ski lifts on the other side of the mountain, their lines running down toward a valley of impenetrable fog.

I was still thinking about Flange's questions—about whether I had doubts about God. I had more doubts, of course, than I cared to admit; and they had more to do with my father than I cared to admit.

He died almost ten years ago. It happened in October, while he was staying at a cottage north of the city. The evening was cold and he had turned on a kerosene-powered heater in the cellar. The unit didn't function properly; the windows of the cottage were closed and carbon monoxide filled up the room where he was sleeping. His brain cells, starved of oxygen, would have started dying within minutes, although his body wasn't discovered until later that day. It would have been a simple tragedy, a death I would have mourned and gotten over, except that he was found naked, in the arms of a woman. A woman who was not my mother.

Until then, I had always looked up to him. He was the strong and reliable type, a structural engineer with a crewcut and rocket-wing nose, a man who occupied himself with stability and foundations. More than anyone in my life he taught me about God: God's power and grace, and God's commandments.

If I began attending church more often after his death, it wasn't simply because of the grief or the shock of the betrayal. It was because I was struggling to separate my father on earth, so to speak, from my Father in heaven. They had become unconsciously fused during my childhood, as if they were the same thing: a father who was God, and a God who had a crewcut. They were like two puzzles whose pieces had become mixed in a single box. Now the pieces had to be examined one by one and set in their proper places. I had never quite managed it, even after all these years. I was still hurting, still disappointed in both of them: in my father for betraying us, and in God for allowing it to happen.

And for allowing him to die.

There was a boom—a fighter jet in the distance. They trained over the mountains, apparently. I walked back to the gondola station and caught the next car down the mountain. Descending, I noticed the cliff again and the path that ran along its edge to the Pfannli.

After exiting the gondola in the village I wandered through the chalets and found my way to the path. It branched off a paved lane and wound into a meadow. To my left were three or four chalets; to my right, emerging out of the grassy earth, was a splinter of grey rock. It tilted upward and became a shelf of rock a few metres above the meadow, and then continued sloping upward while the meadow fell away.

I was soon making my way along a cliff edge several stories high. In this age of legal liability and calculated risk, it was a wonder nobody had built a railing along the precipice. A slight misstep and you were gone—plummeting into a bed of rocks below, or (if you were fortunate) smashing into branches or slamming into a patch of grass, or some painful combination of these.

I reached the waterfall. The stream that fed it was shallow and no more than a footstep wide, murmuring out of the wooded slope. It cut across the path and pooled in a stony pan-shaped basin near the precipice and then spilled off the cliff; hence the name of the waterfall, the Pfannli, or 'Little Pan'. There were footsteps in the mud around the basin and small holes, probably from hiking sticks. I couldn't help wonder if some of these belonged to Sir Kenneth. His final steps.

The peaceful clatter of the falls rose up from below. I peered over the edge and saw the pool, partially obscured by the protrusion of rock near the bottom. He must have fallen from about where I was standing. Further along the cliff wall were the steps he had climbed, and across the meadow was the Iselin. I could see my balcony. A couple of guests were chatting on the balcony above.

I peered over the precipice, further now. A shot of

dread went through me and I felt an urge to jump. I had no wish to end my life, of course, but there was something irresistible about looking down from a great height and wondering what it might be like to lean a little further, to feel my centre of gravity wavering, to risk the unthinkable. That was when I glimpsed a flash in the branches of a bush that sprouted from the cliff wall—the glimmer of a necklace, it seemed.

Stepping back, I lingered for a minute, pondering this odd discovery. A necklace tangled in a branch; a branch under the spot where he fell. Did it have anything to do with Sir Kenneth? Was it worth retrieving the thing? Was it worth risking my neck for it? Curiosity is one of the world's great assassins, and I had no wish to be another victim. And yet I could not resist.

After another cautious glance over the cliff, I sprawled out on my stomach. With one hand gripping the edge of the water basin, I shifted toward the precipice and slipped my free hand over the edge. The cliff wall was jagged, snagging on my sleeve. I slid my groping fingers further down and felt the brush of a leaf. I prodded delicately about some branches until I felt it: a slender chain.

Grabbing hold, I drew it out slowly, carefully, so as not to snap it. But it was not tangled and came away easily. I slid back from the precipice and examined it. It was indeed a necklace. Although unfortunately broken near the clasp, it had an intriguing little watch hanging from it. It was heart-shaped, small as a penny, with the tiniest of arms.

I wiped a droplet off the glass. I took the phone out of my pocket and checked the local time. It was almost five thirty. The watch was set at eleven thirty, six hours behind—or six hours ahead. I put it to my ear and it was ticking.

SEVEN

For the first time, I seriously wondered if Sir Kenneth's death wasn't an accident. Had somebody pushed him—somebody wearing the necklace? Had Sir Kenneth grabbed it at the last moment, snapping it off the neck of his killer while going over the edge?

The prospect was so outlandish that I warned myself not to get carried away. There were any number of ways the watch could have ended up here; it might not have anything to do with Sir Kenneth. I slipped it into my pocket and went to the cliff steps. Taking hold of the rope railing, I descended to the meadow.

I passed my balcony on the corner of the building and became aware of a lulling melody as I continued along the length of the south wing; a chorus of voices drifting in the air. The voices grew louder as I rounded the corner of the wing.

I climbed the steps of the hotel porch and saw that more guests had arrived, although they were not the ones singing. They were standing at the edge of the porch, gazing across the road.

There, along the sides of a low grassy hill, a crowd of about fifty people were gathered, many of them standing with their arms raised to the sky, and facing them at the foot of the hill was a long-haired man in a black vest whose arms were also raised. The hymn was in German but I recognized it:

> Amazing grace, how sweet the sound
> That saved a wretch like me.
> I once was lost but now am found
> Was blind, but now I see.

So the anti-conference had begun. A shudder of unease went through me. Didn't I belong there, among the faithful—even if they were 'fundamentalists'? What was I doing here among the atheists?

Or did I belong anywhere?

I entered the hotel. There were more guests in the lobby and the café, lounging on chairs and looking out the open windows across the road. The Oxford volunteers had set up their memorial on a table at the back of the lobby next to the conference registration booth. Books and framed photos were set out on the table, with smaller pictures fixed to a display board. The woman with the Ovaries button was stationed between the table and booth, and caught my eye as I approached.

'Are you with the conference?' she asked.

'Yes, I am. I've already registered.'

'Would you mind signing our guestbook?'

As she opened it before me, I noticed one of the photos on the display board. It was a close-up shot of Sir Kenneth on the hotel porch, writing on a blue-rimmed sheet that was pressed against his knee. Blakey and Flange were visible in the middle ground, standing over giant chess pieces.

Below this photo was another one, of Sir Kenneth with Leo Granger. The picture had been taken in the café—the self-serve coffee machine was visible behind them. Granger's hiking shoes and shirt had thick reflector lines that caught the flash of the camera as if a bolt of electricity were running through him; but the flash also illuminated a scrap of paper, partly unfolded, in Sir Kenneth's hand. The paper had a blue rim, like the one in the first photo.

'The guestbook,' the Ovaries woman said, offering a pen.

'Thank you.'

'Be sure to write down where you're from as well.'

As I proceeded to sign, I noticed the signature of another guest above my own. James something from Auckland, New Zealand.

I turned to the first page and scanned through the names and places that people had written down. They had come from all over the world. I flipped to the second page. 'What are you doing?' the Ovaries woman said.

'Are you asking everybody at the conference to sign

this book?'

'Everyone who registers.'

I flipped through the remaining pages, continuing to examine the names and countries. Then I returned to my room, put on some fresh clothes, and headed back to the dining hall. The place was almost full and buzzing with conversation.

Flange, Blakey, and Delia were already at our table. I got my salad from the buffet and took my seat across from Delia. She had sultry eyes and smooth shoulder-length hair that hung on either side of her face like a pair of limp red wings. Her blouse was tight, accentuating her bosom, and I told myself not to look, but I looked.

'They're probably praying for Ken's soul,' she said, peering out the window toward the grassy hill. The singing had ended; a balding man was now standing in the midst of the crowd with his head lowered and one hand valiantly raised.

'Let them pray if it comforts them,' Flange said.

'If they needed comfort they could drink whiskey—if any was available in this place.' She looked at me: 'Why is it that evangelicals don't drink, but Catholics do? You're Catholic, aren't you?'

'Conner is Anglican,' Flange said.

'Anglican. I didn't realize. Anglican is as good as atheist nowadays, isn't it?'

'It depends on which Anglican you ask,' I said. 'As for me, I'm not an atheist.'

'So you believe in God.'

'Yes.'

'And you have come to give a talk at an atheist conference.'

'Yes.'

'*That* is courage.'

'Conner is here as a researcher, not a preacher,' Flange said.

'But it must be painful for you to be in our presence?' she said to me.

'Why should it be painful?'

'You're in a hotel full of God-haters.'

'You cannot hate what you don't believe in.'

'He's got you there,' Blakey grinned.

'Shut up, Blakey. You're in a hotel full of *idea-of-God* haters, then.'

'I don't think they're all hateful,' I said.

'Do you have unconscious doubts? Is that why you're here?'

'What is this, the Inquisition?' Flange said.

'It's just a question.'

'I don't have unconscious doubts,' I said. 'All my doubts are conscious. Faith includes uncertainty.'

'So you have doubts, but you believe despite them?'

'Faith is not all about belief. Often it's about trusting even when you don't believe.'

'You mean like blind trust?'

'I mean the way a child trusts in a parent. If a parent tells a child that they'll be visiting a place called Switzerland, the child trusts the parent even if the child has never heard of Switzerland or doubts the existence of Switzerland. The child believes in Switzerland because the child trusts that the parent is not a liar.'

'That's a quaint analogy, except we're not children. We're adults.'

'Enough shop talk,' Flange said.

'There is no evidence of God,' Delia went on. 'No true experimental evidence.'

'In matters of faith, your life is the experiment,' I said. 'And God's hand is the test tube. You drop yourself into it. It involves risk and doubt and being vulnerable. Sometimes the experiment hurts, although if you stay with it, then you might find the evidence.'

'Give me a break. If faith is an experiment, then the experiment is clearly a failure. The history of the world is proof of that. Look at all the wars and violence in the name of religion.'

'Is that proof of God's failure, or our failure?'

'It's the failure of people who use their beliefs to justify killing.'

'Then it is not God's failure. Atheists always assume the problem of evil has something to do with God, forgetting that God made us free to choose.'

'There is no God!' she snapped. It was so sudden that it surprised her as much as it did me. She sat back, glancing about with embarrassment as guests from the nearby tables looked over.

'Please,' Flange said quietly. 'That's enough.'

EIGHT

I WAS ALMOST as ashamed as she was for the outburst, knowing I'd helped to trigger it. There was no further discussion about God, and Delia barely looked at me for the remainder of the meal.

Flange and I went out to the hotel porch afterward. The assembly across the road had thinned to a couple dozen people. The long-haired preacher in the black vest was back again, standing in their midst and sermonizing, waving his hand about like a wand.

'Don't let Delia's reaction trouble you,' Flange said. 'My advice is to avoid any discussions about your personal beliefs while you're here. People will assume you're a fanatic, like those fundamentalists over there. Then again, atheists can be just as fanatical, and sometimes more. Not believing in God can be harder than believing in God. Sometimes you've got to dig your heels in to stay convinced—unconvinced, I should say.'

I noticed Leo Granger sitting on one of the outdoor

couches with a woman. She was talking with him and typing on a laptop. 'Who's that with Leo?' I said.

'She's with the BBC. A nosy little gargoyle with the teeth of a horse, and the breath too. Absurdly polite. She had been planning to do an in-depth piece on Ken, but now that he's gone Leo is the closest she can get.'

'Did they know each other a long time, Sir Kenneth and Leo?'

'They go back quite a few years. It was Leo who convinced Ken to come and work at Mount Albert. He actually wooed him away from Oxford.'

'How did he manage that?'

'Shrewd bargaining. Leo knows a lot of people at the university. They offered Ken a generous salary, and a beautiful office overlooking a forest behind campus. But the biggest selling point was the teaching load, which was almost nil.'

'Meaning he would have a lot of freedom.'

'Exactly. It was an academic's dream, and fortunately Ken couldn't resist. He ended up doing some of his best research at Mount Albert. He and Leo worked well together. Did you read about the aspirin study? It was just published. They gave aspirin to religious extremists and showed that it reduced their level of extremism, apparently because it alleviated some sort of unconscious pain. Isn't that brilliant?'

'Aspirin reduces extremism? Does that mean we should flood the Middle East with painkillers?'

'Yes,' Flange laughed. 'And we'll send bottles of

codeine to the Vatican.'

A pink light was glowing on the slopes of the Grüneggli. The preacher thrust his finger toward the hotel and I caught the sound of his voice. He was speaking in English but had a German accent. 'Vee must love zem! Zey are sinners, but vee must love zem. Vee must love za sinner but hate za sin!'

'Love the sinner and hate the sin,' Flange said. 'A fine piece of advice. How do you love and hate at the same time? It's like tapping your head while rubbing your belly.'

I slipped the heart watch out of my pocket. 'I wanted to ask you about this,' I said.

'What is it?'

'I found it on the cliff. A watch necklace. It was caught in some branches under the precipice.'

Flange looked at it, squinting. 'A pretty trinket. Does it work?'

'Yes, it's ticking. I wonder if it might be of some importance?'

'Importance to what?'

'His death.'

'What? Are you kidding?'

'It was right under the spot where he must have fallen.'

'Conner, please. Somebody obviously dropped it.'

'But why there? And the chain is broken.'

'Maybe that's *why* they dropped it. Who knows, maybe it was a magpie? They steal small shiny objects, don't they?'

'A magpie?'

'I'm simply saying there's probably a mundane explanation—although I can see how it's tempting to make something of it. You find something odd where a man dies and you figure they're connected. The human mind is always connecting dots, even when they don't deserve to be.'

NINE

I DIDN'T PRESS the matter any further, not wanting to annoy him. And I could see his point: the mind looks for patterns. It can find butterflies in inkblots and faces in clouds. Still, the heart watch nagged at me, and there was one possibility that I couldn't resist investigating—assuming she wouldn't lash out at me again.

I slept in the next morning and was late for breakfast. The opening address began immediately afterward. The main conference room was packed, with guests standing in the aisles and media people in the front with cameras. I helped the Oxford volunteers carry in some extra chairs from the lobby and managed to squeeze myself into a spot near the door.

The room lights dimmed, and a spotlight thickened around Leo Granger. He welcomed the group and began speaking about the shock and sadness everyone was feeling over Sir Kenneth's death.

'As tragic as this loss is,' he said, 'Ken would not have

wanted any prayers or hymns. He would have wanted us to remember who he was and the good he accomplished.'

There was a burst of applause. Granger went on to summarize Sir Kenneth's life, recounting what many of us already knew: that he was born to a Jewish father and Catholic mother who had given up on religion after the Second World War; that he had excelled early in school; that he had begun his career as a mathematician, and then drifted into biology, and cognitive science, with forays into philosophy; that he had been knighted for his influential scholarship on morality and compassion; that he was a bestselling author and universally respected, even by his enemies.

'Religious people often asked Ken, "If there is no God, then where does our goodness come from?" And Ken's answer was always the same: "It comes from us!"'

Cheers erupted. Granger thrust a hand toward a photo on the overhead showing Sir Kenneth having tea with Nelson Mandela. People were on their feet clapping.

'And Ken would say that our goodness has *always* come from us. When the churches nursed the sick and fed the poor and gave hope to the hopeless, it was not God who gave these comforts. It was *us*! It was *our* hands and *our* efforts! Wherever there has been hope, and empathy, and encouragement, it has always been given by one person to another.'

Delia Stoltz was a few rows ahead of me. She got up and started toward the door. After a few moments I rose and went out, and as I reached the lobby I spotted her at the end of the corridor leading to the south wing.

She went through a pair of double doors and I walked briskly after her. Her room was on the second floor; Flange had mentioned it. I hurried up the stairwell and caught up to her just as she was about to enter. A maid was vacuuming down the hall.

'Delia!' I called out over the hum of the machine.

She turned, startled at my sudden appearance. 'What do you want?'

I took the watch out of my pocket. 'Is this yours?'

She stared at it. 'No, it isn't.'

'I found it outside. I thought it might be yours.'

'And why would you think that?'

'It's a woman's watch. It was meant to be worn as a necklace.'

'It could be any woman's.'

'The time is six hours behind, or possibly six ahead. That means somebody from the eastern time zone or an Asian time zone brought it here, forgetting to reset the hour to local time—which is understandable. It's such a little thing. Anyway, you were only one of fourteen women I could think of who it might belong to.'

'Only fourteen?' she said wryly, raising her pretty brows.

'The Oxford volunteers have a guestbook. They're making everybody sign it. Name and country. There are eleven women from the eastern time zone and two from the Asian.'

'That's thirteen—and why pick on me?'

'Because you were one of the first to arrive, after Sir Kenneth's wife. She's the fourteenth.'

'The watch might belong to a man. Did you ever think of that?'

'I did—a male atheist cross-dressing scientist. But it seemed somehow unlikely.'

She gave a little smile. 'You never know. Atheists are open-minded about everything. Except God, of course.'

'I'm sorry to have troubled you.'

'Wait,' she said before I could go. 'That was a cheap shot. I shouldn't have said that.'

'You feel strongly about what you believe. I understand.'

'And I should apologize about yesterday. I don't usually shout at people.'

'There are no hard feelings. Anyway, I'm as much to blame. Those kinds of discussions always end up in head-on collisions. Occupational hazard, right?'

'That's true. Maybe we should wear hockey helmets next time?'

'And mouth guards.'

We were silent a moment, grinning, the vacuum humming nearby. 'What did you think of Leo's talk?' I said.

'Honestly? I couldn't stand it. It was like a sermon, the way he carried on.'

'Yes, he was a bit over the top.'

'He was *way* over. So triumphant. I would rather honour Ken by reading his books or talking about his ideas. Have you read any of his writing? *The Probabilities of Life* is his best work.'

'I've read it twice, actually.'

'Really? What was your favourite part?'

'The last chapter. On the beauty of chance.'

'The beauty of chance—I've always loved that line.'

'He had a way with words, didn't he? Whether or not you agreed with him.'

She glanced toward the maid, who was nearing with the machine. 'It's a bit noisy out here. Listen, do you want to come in for a minute? We could chat on the balcony. I was going to take a break before getting back to work.'

'Sure. I suppose I have some time.'

There was a faint smell of cigarettes and perfume in her room. Her bed was unmade. She took a bottle of mineral water and two glasses from a shelf and I followed her outside. Her balcony, like mine, looked toward the meadow and the Pfannli.

'It's a fine view,' I said.

'It's gorgeous. Mind if I smoke?'

'Feel free.'

We settled around a patio table. She poured the mineral water.

'So when is your talk?' she said.

'Thursday morning.'

'What's the topic?'

'How belief in God influences moral behaviour.'

'Ah, the study of sin. What did you find?'

'Well, in a nutshell, my research showed that religious

people are less likely to cheat on a task when they believe in a punishing God, and more likely to cheat when they believe in a forgiving God.'

'So hell is more persuasive than heaven?'

'It would seem so.'

'That won't inspire many new converts, you realize?'

'I know. But fortunately I'm not a preacher.'

She laughed.

'And your research?' I said. 'What's it about?'

'Let me start by asking you a question. Imagine that you go to a store to buy a baseball bat and a ball. The bat and the ball cost one dollar and ten cents in total. The bat costs one dollar more than the ball. The question is, how much does the ball cost?'

I sipped my water. 'Five cents. If the ball is five cents, then the bat is a dollar five, which is a dollar more.'

She smiled, tapping her cigarette against the ashtray. 'Well done. Many people think the answer is ten cents.'

'What was the point of the question?'

'I wanted to see if you were analytically minded or intuitively minded. People who think intuitively tend to get the answer wrong. They go with their gut and say ten cents. But people who are analytically minded resist going with their gut. They're more likely to consider the information rationally. Analytically minded people are also less likely to believe in God.'

'Then I must be an exception, since I believe in God. Do you want to ask me the question again? I could give you the wrong answer this time, if you prefer.'

'You might make an interesting case study.'

'So is this what you do in your research? Torment people with mathematics?'

'We took a group of people who were very religious, and we trained them to think analytically using math. A few hours of math training resulted in a small but measurable increase in their doubts about God.'

'You mean learning algebra could undermine religion?'

'You figured out my scheme.'

I became aware of a baby crying. It was coming from somewhere in the meadow. Delia exhaled a plume of smoke. 'I hope this isn't bothering you?' she said, indicating the cigarette.

'I'm okay. Enjoy your vice.'

'What about you? Do you have any vices?'

'Absolutely. I'm a glutton for knowledge.'

'How depraved.'

'Oh, you learn to live with it. Where is that cry coming from?'

She nodded in the direction of the cliff. I leaned forward and saw a woman walking through the grass carrying a baby in a sling.

'She takes him out whenever he cries,' Delia said. 'I think she's from the pension next door.'

'Pension?'

'The guesthouse.'

The woman passed the bottom of the cliff steps and then turned and paced the other way. 'Does she ever walk the baby in the morning?' I asked.

'Yes. Haven't you heard it?'

'I'm a heavy sleeper.'

There was a raspy squawking in the meadow.

'I hear that a lot too,' she said.

'It's a magpie. There, with the black and white plumage. He's hopping in the grass. And there's a cat watching him from the corner of that chalet.'

As she sat up and peered over the railing, I glanced toward the cliff, at the cluster of branches where I'd found the watch, wondering if Flange was right. Anybody could have dropped it there—including a magpie. I felt suddenly like a fool with all my suspicions.

'You know, you would have liked Ken,' Delia said. 'He was observant, as you seem to be.'

'Who'll be your supervisor now that he's gone?'

'It's hard to say. Leo is the only other person in the department doing the same sort of research, but there's no way I'd work with him.'

'Flange seems to have had a good experience with him.'

'Because Flange is an oddball. Sorry, I know he's your friend.' The crying of the baby grew louder. Delia muttered something in annoyance and then mashed her cigarette in the ashtray. 'Let me ask you another question. A religious question. I want your honest opinion. I won't be offended.'

'Alright.'

'Do you think that Ken is still alive somewhere? I

mean, in the unlikely event—the very unlikely event—that there is a heaven, would Ken be allowed in?'

'It would depend.'

'On what? Whether he believed in the Bible?'

'No. It would depend on the condition of his heart. It might depend on more than that, but it would not depend on less.'

'You're saying that an atheist can go to heaven?'

'Yes. But if he did it wouldn't be because of his atheism. It would be in spite of it.'

'That all sounds very nice, but you don't really know, do you?'

'It's as close to the truth as I can get.'

'I think he's gone. Just gone. Like when a light goes out.'

'That must be difficult.'

'It is what it is,' she said with a shrug. 'Although a part of me almost wishes I could believe what you believe. In a God, in a heaven. I'd be happy if I could believe in that, just for a little while.'

'Because it would make things easier?'

'Yes. I don't like the idea that he's lying in a morgue somewhere. That he's just lying there. Decomposing.'

'I know what you mean.'

'Do you?' she said sharply.

'What I meant is...'

'I'm sorry, I wasn't supposed to be offended,' she said, giving her eyes a wipe. 'Anyway, I should be getting to work. I've got my talk this afternoon.'

TEN

AS I STEPPED into the corridor, I noticed the hotel manager. He was at the door of the next room, standing with his hands behind his back. He glanced at me with a tight smile.

I replied in kind and went downstairs to my room. I stood on the balcony and looked toward the cliff wall.

The mother was still walking the infant. She passed the bottom of the cliff steps and walked to the trees, and then she turned and walked the other way, out of sight behind the building. After a minute she reappeared and paced toward the trees and then circled again, and all the while the infant's cry echoed between the hotel and the cliff, at times louder, at times softer.

I hopped over the balcony railing and strode through the grass. She was a petite woman with rings of exhaustion under her eyes.

'Pardon me,' I said. 'I wonder if I might ask you a question?'

'Je ne parle pas anglais,' she said, jiggling the baby.

I followed alongside her and attempted, in the little French I knew, to ask if she had spoken with the police about Sir Kenneth. But it was no use. She didn't understand and didn't seem interested. As I wandered back to my balcony, I glanced up toward Delia's, vaguely hoping to catch her eye. But she had gone back into her room. I hopped over my railing again.

I headed to the hotel lobby. Leo Granger's talk had ended and people were milling about. Flange was at the coffee machine.

'There you are,' he said as I came up. 'I didn't see you. Were you at the talk?'

'I caught part of it. I was at the back.'

'It was well done, don't you think? What everybody needed to hear. Something positive.' He was searching his pockets. 'I need another franc—a coin. This machine only takes coins. Very temperamental. One mistake and it won't cooperate. Yesterday I burned my fingers using a cup to make a latte macchiato when I should have used a glass.'

I found a one-franc piece in my pocket. He slipped it into the machine and pressed a button. The chrome box rumbled and hummed, and hot milk and steam began spurting out. 'Blakey's talk will be starting soon,' he said, checking his watch. 'Are you coming? The topic is death anxiety. It's along the lines of our conversation yesterday, but with a twist.'

'What twist?'

'You'll see. I just hope he doesn't make an ass of himself. Ah look, look at this.' The milk had stopped and the espresso was dribbling out, swirling into the white, pushing up a layer of foam. 'Just beautiful. The perfect latte. If there's one thing I've noticed about Switzerland, it's that there are a lot of rules, although if you follow them then things work exactly as they should.'

There was a commotion behind us. We turned and saw Eleanor Chatwin. She was making her way through the lobby dragging a piece of wheeled luggage. Her face was lowered and the hotel manager was striding beside her, hands clasped behind him. The woman from the BBC and two men, other reporters it seemed, were following and calling out to Eleanor.

'Ms Chatwin! Just a few questions! If we may, please!'

Flange shoved the hot latte into my hands and followed them out the door. People began moving to the windows and trickling out to the porch.

I hurried outside and watched. Flange caught up to Eleanor and got between her and the reporters with his arms raised, trying to keep them back, and then Granger jogged up and joined in the defence. Eleanor's luggage rumbled over the porch with a shirt sleeve hanging out of it, dragging like a tail. As they reached the porch steps Granger picked up the suitcase and carried it down for her. Flange went with them while the manager remained behind, waving back the reporters.

I moved to the porch railing and peered down toward the parking lot; it was a single lane with a row of spaces along it. Granger and Flange walked Eleanor to a small car, a hatchback. She opened the trunk and Granger lifted the suitcase inside. Eleanor unzipped a side pocket and pulled out a sheaf of papers and handed them to Granger.

The three of them spoke briefly, and then Eleanor got into the car and drove away.

The crowd on the porch drifted back into the hotel. Granger and Flange remained in the parking lane sifting through the papers. Flange took some of them, and when he came back up to the porch a few minutes later I waved him over.

'Your latte is cooling off.'

'I hope you didn't sip it?' he said, taking the glass. 'I detest germs when they're not my own.'

'I didn't touch it. What was Eleanor doing here?'

'She was collecting Ken's things. You'd think people would leave her alone at a time like this.'

'You found something of interest?' I said, indicating the rolled up pages in his hand.

'Ken was going to make some edits to my talk. He never got around to it, it seems. Poor Eleanor. I felt like we were plundering her husband's grave.'

'What about Sir Kenneth's talk? The talk he was supposed to give this morning. Did you find it?'

'I didn't see anything in the papers we went through. There were some rough notes, quite illegible.'

'Were they on hotel stationery? The paper with the blue rim.'

'There were a few sheets like that. Why?'

'He was making notes on hotel stationery. I saw it in two of the pictures on the display board in the lobby.'

'Ken was always making notes of some kind.'

'But he must have written down the talk. It must be somewhere.'

'He may not have written anything formal. His mind was encyclopedic. He may have planned to throw something together at the last moment.'

'To improvise?'

'He's done it before, especially when lecturing about grand ideas—which is what he was intending for the opening address. The future of atheism. Why are you so suspicious anyway? You're not trying to connect any more dots, are you?'

'I'm only curious.'

'Good. I was starting to think you were getting paranoid.' He glanced at his watch. 'Time for Blakey now. Shall we go?'

ELEVEN

I'D HARDLY LOOKED at Zach Blakey until his talk that morning. He was so bland and inoffensive that I'd only noticed pieces of him until then. His hair was neatly parted, his forehead wide and smooth, and his grin was shy, buttoned firmly between his cheeks. He wore an olive green shirt that bulged at the belly, and jeans and vintage basketball sneakers—the classic black-and-whites with the high ankles. Altogether, he left you with the impression of an overgrown little boy.

His talk was not well attended. Only a dozen chairs in the seminar room were occupied. The words *Death Anxiety and Atheism* were beamed on the screen behind him.

'According to many philosophers,' he began, 'one of the main occupations of human beings is the fear of death.'

'*Preoccupations*,' somebody called out.'

'Yes, preoccupations.'

'Louder please.'

Blakey leaned into the microphone, breath gushing. 'Death terrifies us because it marks the end of our existence. That was a bit loud. Sorry.'

He adjusted the mike, blinking nervously. Then he touched the laptop. The image of a gravestone appeared on the overhead screen.

'We deal with our anxiety about death by finding ways to deny our mortality,' he said. 'Religion, with its notions of an afterlife, is one way of denying death, but it's not the only way. There are other psychological crutches. We can immerse ourselves in careers, families, and entertainment, all as a way of distracting ourselves from death, and giving us a sense of power, security, and symbolic immortality. Today, I'd like to discuss how atheism itself may be another way of coping with death anxiety—in fact, how atheism may be another form of religion.'

'Nonsense,' grumbled an older man in the front. 'Atheism is not a religion. It is a worldview.'

'Similar idea, I guess.'

'They are quite distinct.'

'Anyway I, uh, conducted my research in collaboration with Sir Kenneth Chatwin. Here's what we did.'

He pressed a button on his laptop and looked up at the screen behind him. The slide didn't change; it was still showing the gravestone.

Flange leaned toward me: 'Ken didn't have anything

to do with this study. He was still recovering from the stroke when Blakey set it up. Ken approved it, but I doubt he knew what he was approving.'

Blakey cleared his throat and started fiddling with the laptop, but the slide remained stuck on the gravestone. Two people gathered up their things and left the room.

'I was with Delia earlier,' I whispered to Flange.

'With Delia? What are you talking about?'

'I was in her room.'

'That's a bit risqué, don't you think?'

'Nothing happened. We talked about our research.'

'And how did this intriguing encounter arise?'

'Do you recall the watch I found yesterday? I thought it might be hers. She said it wasn't but invited me inside.'

'You and your suspicions!'

'I just needed to be sure.'

'As for Delia, you should be careful with her. She's bright and beautiful, there's no denying that, but she's also manipulative and controlling. You should see her in lab meetings. Loves to dominate. Unless you like domination?' he chuckled, giving me an elbow.

'I'm naïve about that sort of thing.'

'We'll see how long that lasts. Just keep my opinions about her strictly confidential. I don't want to get on her bad side.'

'I didn't say I was seeing her again.'

'You will, if you're a fool—even a bit of a fool. Which every man is.'

Blakey was still tinkering with his laptop. 'This is

getting embarrassing,' I whispered.

'Let him suffer. He needs to learn how to manage stress. Blakey's a bit soft and bumbling, in case you haven't noticed. He's had problems with alcohol too. That's confidential as well, mind you.'

'Alcohol? Are you serious?'

'He's sober now, as far as I understand, but he was in an awful state last year.'

'How do you know all this?'

'It was impossible not to know. He'd show up to lab meetings with booze on his breath. We were at a conference in Philadelphia and he stumbled into Ken's seminar, incoherent and raving. The university forced him to take a semester off and get rehab. He came back in September, cleaned up it seemed, although by then Ken had had his stroke and there was nobody to supervise him. Leo was supposed to help out until Ken got better, but he left Blakey on his own for the most part. That's when Blakey set up the study. It's badly designed, as you'll see in a moment, if he can ever fix that machine. Ken eventually realized what a shoddy job he'd done, but in the end he decided to let him present it here. Ken felt sorry for him, I think.'

'So Blakey's sober now?'

'Well, you never really know with addicts, do you? They're experts at hiding things. I'm sure he struggles with the temptation. Speaking of which, I still can't believe you were in Delia Stoltz's room.'

'You're quite scandalized by this, aren't you?'

'She's manipulative and controlling—mark my words. On top of that, she's an atheist and you're a believer. You'd be at each other's throats. Have you already forgotten how she blew up at you yesterday?'

TWELVE

BLAKEY'S LAPTOP REVIVED at last. He pushed on with the talk, but an atmosphere of irritation had settled on the audience, and his fumbling delivery did nothing to improve the mood. People interrupted him, challenging his logic, his method, his statistics. He blinked and grimaced and adjusted his glasses as if darts were being thrown into his face.

The talk ended early. We went up to him afterward and Flange tried to encourage him, saying it went pretty well, but Blakey wasn't fooled. He packed up his things quickly, glassy-eyed, and left the room.

'You see,' Flange said pitifully. 'Too soft.'

He invited me to join him at another seminar but I wasn't in the mood. I made a latte in the café, sat at the window, and thought about Delia.

I had followed her up to her room to ask about the heart watch, but I admitted, now, that was only a half-truth. An excuse to get closer to her.

I'd been attracted to her from the beginning. It wasn't only her looks, sultry and beguiling as they were. It was that she saw the world so differently than I did. That sparked a fresh impulse in me. A wild little wish to escape into something new.

I warned myself to ignore it. She wasn't right for me—our differences were too great—and Flange's opinion only reinforced that conclusion. Did I really want to get closer to somebody who was *manipulative* and *controlling*?

Then again, opinion wasn't always reality, especially in human relationships.

Anyway, how could I even be sure that *she* had any interest in me?

And yet, I had sensed something.

I finished my latte. It was too early for lunch and I went back to my room and turned on the TV. It was the second day of Wimbledon and the sports news was doing a special feature on the Swiss favourite—a veteran and former champion who'd crushed his opponents with pinpoint forehands and cunning drop shots. A game of pure genius.

A thing of beauty.

I thought of Delia with a faint wave of longing. I went out to the balcony and looked up toward her room. I inhaled the air trying to catch a whiff of her cigarettes. I went back inside and watched TV for a while longer and then realized it was almost noon. She may have already gone for lunch.

I checked my hair and adjusted my shirt and hurried to the dining hall. The place was filling up but she wasn't there. Neither were Flange or Blakey. Our table was empty and Leo Granger was at another table on the other side of the hall.

I filled my plate at the salad bar. A dead fly was floating in the French dressing. I sat alone and the milk-maid waitress came gliding toward me. She was beautiful too, I admitted, but it was a different kind of beauty. Too pure to touch.

'Will your friends be coming?' she said.

'I expect they should be. Professor Granger is over there,' I said, gesturing in his direction.

'Oh,' she said. 'The one with the beard?'

'Yes.'

A ripple of consternation passed across her immaculate face. She thanked me and walked to the doors of the kitchen and spoke to another waiter, pointing out Granger. The waiter nodded. He wove through the tables up to Granger and leaned over with a polite smile. Words were exchanged, and Granger looked behind his chair with a frown.

Evidently the chair, which he had squeezed up to the table, had created an obstruction. Granger pulled the chair closer to the table while his colleagues shifted over, but the waiter was unsatisfied with this solution. He pointed toward me.

Granger got up and walked over with his plate, shaking his head. 'These people and their rules,' he muttered, taking his seat.

'They're Swiss,' I said. 'They're particular about rules.'

He jabbed the fork into his salad and stuffed it into his mouth. I expected him to remain aloof, as he usually was with me, but after a little silence he said, with a grumble, 'So why are you here?'

'Here?'

'At a conference for atheists.'

'Everybody seems to be asking me that question. I'm giving a talk on—'

'I know what you're giving a talk on. But you're not an atheist. You believe in God.'

'Which gives me a great deal in common with atheists. We are both obsessed with the same thing, just in opposite ways.'

He gave a dim laugh.

'And I respect atheists,' I said, sounding a more serious note. 'They often ask more interesting questions than people who believe in God.'

'That's because atheists ask questions when they don't already have an answer. When an atheist asks *What is the origin of life?* he's genuinely wondering. He doesn't know and is searching for information. When a religious person asks *What is the origin of life?* he's not asking a question. He already knows the answer based on what he's read in the Bible or some other holy book. He's only asking the question as a lead-in to a sermon. There's no real curiosity behind it.'

The milk maid arrived with bowls of soup. Granger

watched her as she went off, his gaze wandering down her backside.

'Strictly speaking, I wouldn't describe myself as religious,' I said. 'People think that believing in God is about following certain rules, like going to church every Sunday. But it isn't about rules. It's not even about beliefs. Not fundamentally.'

'Then what is it about?'

'It's about the heart. It's about where the heart is in relationship to God.'

'Ah yes. *The Lord is nigh unto them that are of a broken heart.*'

I beheld him with faint astonishment. He seemed suddenly a prophet with his dark beard and solemn eyes.

'Psalm 34, if I recall,' he said. 'I was raised in a religious family.'

'I had no idea.'

'I probably know the Bible better than some of the people across the road. I also learned something else growing up. These people claim to follow a God of love but they secretly hate anybody who isn't like them. They'll shake your hand and smile while mentally damning you to hell.'

He uttered that remark harshly, and it almost silenced me. But now that I'd gotten him talking I couldn't resist delving further.

'What kind of church did your family belong to?' I asked.

'It was a tight-knit evangelical group. Almost a cult. I

wasn't allowed to play with children outside the church. I was homeschooled and my exposure to books was controlled—until I was fifteen.'

'Why fifteen?'

'That was when a little miracle happened. I discovered a book in my neighbour's trash bin. A psychology textbook. I took it out of the bin and read it in the woods at the back of our house. I hid it there, and each day after lunch I would go out and immerse myself in it. The book was years out of date but it was a revelation to me. Have you heard of Watson's experiments with Little Albert?'

'The classical conditioning study with the baby?'

'Yes. As you might recall, the experimenters showed Little Albert a white rat and at first he wasn't afraid to touch it. Then they clanged a hammer against a bar whenever he reached for the rat, and of course that made Albert afraid. But the fear also became associated with the rat itself, so that he began to fear the rat even when they didn't hit the bar. They say that Little Albert even developed a fear of other furry objects, like dogs and rabbits and a Santa Claus outfit. It was fear by association, you see. I realized it was a symbol for my life.'

'You mean your parents had taught you to be afraid of everything.'

'It wasn't my parents. It was their religion. Their religion had drawn a circle, a very small circle, in which everything inside the circle was good, and everything outside the circle was evil and frightening. I was Little

Albert, and their religion was the hammer clanging against the world.'

'Did they ever find out about the book?'

'Not before I'd read it from cover to cover a couple of times. And in the meantime I discovered other books. Whenever I put out the garbage in the evening I would walk up and down the road, checking everybody else's trash. I found a biography of Edison, a history of China, Dostoyevsky's *Crime and Punishment*. I even found a Spiderman comic. Now that was a revelation!'

He gave an easy laugh, without the usual gloom, and I laughed with him. For a moment I almost liked him.

'I hid the books under a boulder in the forest,' he went on. 'Eventually my parents found them and burned them, right in our backyard. I watched the fire from my bedroom window. I tell you, I got a good beating that day, but it didn't matter. I was free. The books were ashes but the ideas were alive in my head.'

'I can understand your distrust of religion. Given your experiences.'

'At least those experiences taught me the truth. Belief in God is a kind of delusion.'

'You mean the truth as you know it.'

'No, it's not the truth as I know it. It doesn't only belong to me and a special group. It belongs to everyone. Everyone who can *reason*, that is,' he added with an emphatic sting.

'So reason is your God?' I said, taking the bait.

'Metaphorically, yes. And reason was Ken's God, and

the God of everyone in this room. Do you think we're fools because we use logic before we'll believe something?'

'I don't think you're fools. But if I believe there might be limits to logic, does that make me *primitive*?'

He glared at me, shoulders heaving as he took a fuming breath through his beard. I shouldn't have said 'primitive'. It was mean and petty, recalling his remark the night that Sir Kenneth got angry with him.

Flange, fortunately, was hurrying toward the table just then. He was holding a smartphone.

'Leo, we have a slight problem,' he said.

'What problem?'

He held out the phone. The screen showed a newspaper headline: *Famous Atheist Had Affair With Student*. Underneath it were photos of Sir Kenneth and Delia Stoltz.

THIRTEEN

SIR KENNETH'S PICTURE was the same charming image that appeared in yesterday's news story about his death, but Delia's shot was quite different: she gazed past the camera as if unaware of it, or indifferent to it, her eyes shadowy and seductive, her lips parted.

I stared at the screen, stunned. 'Malcolm noticed the story a few minutes ago,' Flange whispered.

'Who the hell is Malcolm?' Granger said.

'Malcolm from Oxford.' Flange glanced over his shoulder. The scruffy-headed young man and the Ovaries woman were in the doorway, watching us.

Granger got up and Flange gestured for me to follow. We walked out to the lobby where Malcolm scrolled through several newspaper headlines on his tablet. 'The story has spread quickly,' he said. 'It seems to have originated in the Chronicle. It's a British tabloid. They said they had a source.'

Granger turned to me with a menacing look.

‘What?’ I said. ‘I have nothing to do with this.’

The woman from the BBC came up. ‘Professor Granger, are you aware of today’s story about Sir Kenneth and Ms Stoltz?’

‘Jeremy, let’s go,’ he said.

Flange again gestured for me to follow. We headed down the corridor and went through the double doors into the south wing.

‘What room is she in?’ Granger said.

‘She’s on the second floor,’ Flange said. ‘The room next to Ken’s.’

Granger looked at me. ‘Why is he following us?’

‘Because Conner spoke with Delia this morning.’

‘I thought you had nothing to do with this?’

‘I don’t.’

‘Wait here. Both of you.’ Granger went into the stairwell and we watched his figure through the frosted glass as he went bounding up the steps.

‘I told you she was trouble,’ Flange said.

‘You said she was manipulative and controlling. You didn’t say she was sleeping with Sir Kenneth.’

‘I did mention that she loves to dominate, didn’t I?’

I took out my phone and found the article:

> Sir Kenneth Chatwin, the renowned atheist, had a sexual affair with one of his students, an anonymous source has informed the Chronicle. The alleged affair between the aging Chatwin and Delia Stoltz, aged twenty-six, reportedly led to an abortion at a

> Toronto clinic in May of this year.
>
> Chatwin, who died yesterday in Switzerland, had been knighted for his research on morality and is the author of the critically acclaimed book, *The Probabilities of Life*. An outspoken critic of religion, he spent many years at the University of Oxford and most recently held a position at Mount Albert University near Toronto, where he was helping to organize a Humanist Studies Program.
>
> The University declined to comment on the allegations of the affair, but released the following statement: "At this time we are grieving the loss of a great mind, and remembering his extraordinary contributions to the advancement of psychological science."
>
> Chatwin, aged sixty-three, was married and had no children. He had been in Switzerland preparing for a major conference when he unexpectedly died after falling from a clifftop. Swiss authorities informed the Chronicle that they are treating his death as an accident. They had no comment on the allegations of the affair.

Granger returned. 'She's not in her room. Do you have her phone number?'

'I've already called her,' Flange said. 'She's not answering.'

'Call her again.' He unlocked his door and led us inside.

His room was on a corner, like mine, but on the other side of the wing, with the bed and other furniture in opposite positions.

'So you spoke with her this morning?' he said to me.

'Yes. We chatted for a few minutes.'

'Are you involved with her?'

'No, of course not. I simply wanted to ask her about a watch I had found.'

'What watch?'

I slipped it out of my pocket. 'I found this yesterday. I thought it might be hers.'

He studied it for a moment. 'What happened then?'

'As I said, we just chatted.'

'Did she talk about Ken?'

'A little, although she didn't say anything about being involved with him. She did get tearful at one point.'

'Tearful?'

'There was nothing suspicious about it. She just seemed sad that he was gone.'

'Wait,' Flange said. 'She wept in front of you?'

'I didn't say wept, I said tearful.'

'Well, well. And I thought she was cold as ice.'

'Give me your phone,' Granger said to Flange. 'Where's the article?'

As Granger read through it, I noticed a pile of loose papers on his table. They were face down, with blue-rimmed edges.

'Any idea who this anonymous source might be?' he said.

'No doubt somebody with an axe to grind,' Flange said. 'It could be one of the religious fanatics out there.'

'You're probably right. They're trying to smear his name with lies. This is the last thing we need right now.'

'Actually, it may not be all lies.'

'Meaning what?'

'There may be some truth to the story.'

'Some truth? What do you know about this, Jeremy?'

'Well—'

'What the hell do you know?'

'I did have some suspicions, I suppose. Not that I knew the extent of the situation.'

'The extent of *what* situation?'

'Alright. It began a few months ago.'

'What began? What are you talking about!'

'If you would calm down.'

'You *knew* something and you didn't tell me?'

'I'm telling you now.'

Granger cursed under his breath, shaking his head.

'As I said,' Flange continued, 'it was a few months ago. Back in March. She went into his office one day. It was after hours and there was nobody else on the floor. Nobody except me. I saw her go in but I don't think she knew I was still there. I had meant to talk with Ken about my dissertation. I assumed she had gone to speak with him briefly, so I waited in my office, knowing that I'd hear his door open—the bolt makes a heavy click. After almost an hour I didn't hear anything, and so I went down the hall and noticed the light in his office was still on. I could see it under the crack of the door. I put my ear to the door and I could hear something.'

'You heard what?'

'I heard sounds. The sounds of—you know.'

'Sex.'

'I assume it was that. It sounded like that.'

'This was in March?'

'Yes.'

'And you didn't mention this to anybody?'

'It was hardly my business.'

'Hardly your business? The man wasn't well, Jeremy. He was recovering from a stroke.'

'But he'd already recovered.'

'He had sex with his student! Didn't you think there might be repercussions?'

'Well, I...' Flange said with a helpless shrug.

Granger dug a hand into his beard, clawing irritably. 'So what else do you know?'

'Over the next few weeks I noticed that she would often visit his office after hours. They seemed to have a pattern on Wednesdays and Fridays.'

'A pattern? For weeks? What about the abortion? Is that part true?'

'I don't know. But I do recall she was away for a week in May. That might have been when she decided to do it.'

'Why didn't you mention this!'

'Because I had no idea things may have gone that far—and of what I did know, I simply didn't think it was my business. Who are we to judge him anyway?'

'That's not the point! We're talking about Ken. Sir Kenneth Chatwin! He wasn't just anybody. He has a reputation. *Had* one.'

Granger sighed and leaned over the table, staring down at the blue-rimmed pages.

'Do we call Eleanor?' Flange said quietly.

'Not yet.'

Granger went out to his balcony and began shouting up toward the second floor: 'Stoltz! Stoltz, can you hear me!'

'A disaster,' Flange whispered. 'A bloody disaster.'

'It may be the reason why Eleanor is staying with Margaret,' I said. 'Do you remember what Margaret told me the other day? Eleanor and Sir Kenneth got into an argument on Friday. That was why Eleanor left the hotel. What if she found out about the affair that day? When did Delia arrive?'

'Friday. One day before the rest of us.'

I went to the table and turned up one of the blue-rimmed pages. The writing was messy, but I managed to make out the word *humming*.

'What are you doing?' Flange said, coming up and slapping the page flat.

'Was that Sir Kenneth's?'

'It's private, whatever it is.'

Granger came back inside. 'She's either not there or not answering. Where is Blakey?'

'Don't know,' Flange said. 'I sent him a text.'

'The reporters are going to be all over this. I'll have to

talk to them. I'm going to say there's no proof of it. If they ask you about it—either of you—you don't know anything. Everything we've discussed here is confidential. Do you understand?'

We nodded.

'Isn't Stoltz giving a talk today?'

'She's scheduled for one thirty,' Flange said. 'But I have a feeling she might not show up.'

Granger looked at his watch. 'That's in forty-five minutes. Let's see what happens.'

FOURTEEN

WE HEADED BACK to the lobby with Granger striding before us. People were hunched over laptops and tablets reading the news. I caught the flicker of Delia's alluring gaze on several screens.

I still felt something for her. I couldn't deny it. I felt even more than before, in fact.

Pity and desire—a dangerous mix.

A little band of reporters rushed toward us and beleaguered Granger with questions. He kept to the script, saying there was no evidence of the affair and insisting the story was concocted by Sir Kenneth's enemies.

It wasn't long before the manager shoved his way into the huddle, red-faced and agitated, demanding peace. We slipped into the dining hall and found Blakey alone at the table. He'd gone out to the village after his talk and had just heard the news about Delia and Sir Kenneth.

'It's only a rumour, right?' he said. 'It can't be true.'

‘Of course it’s a rumour,’ Granger said.

The milk maid arrived with our plates, prompt as ever. The main course, roast beef in a Bernese wine sauce, might have been pleasant were it not for the atmosphere. People were talking, glancing at our table. The windows were open and the music of a guitar, the sweet plucking of a hymn, drifted over the hushed conversation.

We finished up quickly and headed to the seminar room where Delia was expected for her talk. The room gradually filled up, but one thirty came and went with no sign of her.

Flange tried her again on his phone. Soon people began to trickle out. Granger and Flange exchanged whispers and got up to leave, and Blakey and I followed. The woman from the BBC was waiting in the corridor.

‘Professor Granger,’ she said. ‘If I may speak with you for a moment.’

Granger ignored her and hurried down the hallway, escaping into one of the other seminar rooms with Flange and Blakey.

I took out my phone. I’d glimpsed Delia’s phone number while Flange was calling her. I tapped out the numbers and sent her a message: *Where are you? Let me help.*

I walked to the south wing and took the stairs to the second floor. I knocked on her door. ‘Delia?’ I called out. ‘Are you there? It’s Conner.’

There was no response.

I went downstairs and out to my balcony, and leaned

over the railing and called up to her room. Nothing. I returned to the lobby and found Blakey by the café window. He was reading a tablet.

'Where are Jeremy and Leo?' I said.

'They're still in the talk. It wasn't all that interesting.'

The tablet was open to the comments section of an article. Somebody had written: *Atheists like Chatwin are immoral! That's why they don't want to believe in God!*

'What are you reading?'

'It's from a fundamentalist website. I wanted to see how people were reacting to the news. It's pretty offensive.'

'Do you think religious people might be behind it?'

He glanced through the window toward the grassy hill. 'It seems to be the popular theory. Assuming the story is even true.'

'If it is true, then somebody very close to Sir Kenneth or Delia must have leaked it.'

'Why do you say that?'

'Consider the details. The bit about the abortion, for instance. That itself is very personal, and we're even told it happened in Toronto, in May. Only somebody close to her, or him, could be aware of all that.'

'Maybe it was somebody at the clinic?'

'I doubt it. People who work at abortion clinics tend to be non-religious and politically liberal, sympathetic to Sir Kenneth's worldview. He wouldn't have enemies there. The other curious detail is the photo of Delia. It looks spontaneous and provocative, and somewhat grainy. The picture could be a selfie. I wouldn't be surprised if somebody hacked into her computer or her phone. It might explain how they got both the photo and the details of the affair. Did you ever suspect anything between them?'

'No. But I suppose you never know what's in people's hearts, right? You see them from the outside, but you never know who they really are.'

'On the subject of hearts,' I said, taking the watch out of my pocket. 'Have you ever seen this before?'

He cupped it in his palm and adjusted his glasses. 'A heart watch,' he said.

'Do you recognize it?'

'Where did you find this?'

'Outside.'

'I haven't seen it before, but—this is weird—somebody did mention a heart watch a few days ago. Do you remember the day before yesterday, the day before Ken died? We were playing pool. Me, Jeremy, and Leo. It was that night.'

'I remember. I had come out for a cup of tea.'

'It was just after that. This boy came running down the hall with a doll in his hands. It was the boy with the loose front tooth.'

'From the German family?'

'Yes. I assume the doll was his sister's. He had this mischievous grin on his face. He stuck the doll in that potted tree by the window and then hid behind the couch. His mother arrived a minute later and found him, and noticed the doll and took it down. She searched the doll's neck and then she said to the boy, "Wo ist die Herz Uhr?" I studied German in undergrad and so I knew what it meant: "Where's the heart watch?" The boy said nothing and she asked him again: "Where did you put that heart watch?" He said he didn't have it. Then she grabbed him by the arm, saying he was a bad child, and took him away.'

'Did Jeremy and Leo see all this too?'

'I don't know if they were paying much attention. They were in the middle of a round of pool. They'd knocked me out of the game. Where did you find the watch?'

'Outside. On the cliff behind the hotel.'

'On the cliff? That doesn't make any sense.'

'No, it doesn't.'

FIFTEEN

I ABANDONED BLAKEY with an abrupt apology and crossed the lobby to the reception desk. 'There is a German family staying here,' I said to the woman on duty. 'They're from Munich. Two kids and their parents. Can you tell me what room they're in?'

'I'm sorry, I cannot share that information.'

'I understand. But I've found something that might belong to them. A personal item. Would you mind ringing their room for me?'

She phoned but there was no answer. 'They must be out for the afternoon,' she said. 'Do you wish to leave the item with me?'

'I'll hold onto it for now.'

I spent the next few minutes wandering around the hotel looking for the Munichs. I checked the corridors and the lower lobby and the spa, and then I went back upstairs, pausing at the billiards table.

The table was tucked into a cozy space where the

corridor bent and widened. It was coin-operated. You put in two Swiss francs, pushed them into the slot, and the balls came thudding out of their chamber and rolled to an opening at the front end of the table.

The couch, a leather two-seater, was positioned at the other end. There was a space a few feet wide between the back of the couch and the wall, which had a radiator running along it. The potted tree was in the corner by a broad window, and further along the window were two wooden chairs beside a rack of cue sticks.

I went behind the couch, and squatted down and looked under it. The floor was tile and hadn't been swept lately; there was a layer of dust.

I got up, and took the watch out of my pocket and looked at the chain. The watch had been on the doll's neck—Frau Munich had searched it—but the boy had probably yanked it off. That was why the chain was broken. But where did he put the watch then? Did he throw it away before running to the billiards area? Did somebody else pick it up? If I could find the boy and his family, I might get closer to what happened.

Not that I could be sure it really mattered. The watch might not have anything to do with Sir Kenneth's death. That was still speculation. But the possibility had a firm grip on me now.

I returned to my room and stuffed a jacket and bottle of water into my pack. I went outside and crossed the road. Much of the crowd on the hill had dissolved since the lunch hour. People were sitting in small groups and talking; some were browsing around tables of books and CDs that were set up around the perimeter of the hill.

A man behind one of the tables grinned as I approached. He had bright eyes and a squashed boxer's nose. An older woman sat beside him knitting.

'You're from the conference?' the man said.

'Yes, I am.'

'Welcome, welcome! These are all free,' he declared, sweeping his hand over the books. 'Take one. Here's the truth about evolution—the things they *won't* teach you in the ivory tower!'

'Don't pressure him, Neville,' the woman said.

'Who's pressuring? I'm only offering him books.'

'My reading list is a bit crowded just now,' I said.

'You're a student, then?'

'I'm doing a PhD in psychology.'

'Excellent! I took a psychology course once. But I will tell you this—nothing makes sense without God. Nothing!'

'You're going to drown the boy in your enthusiasm,' the woman said.

'People need to hear the truth, Mother.'

'Of course. But the truth comes to us in different ways sometimes.'

'Listen,' he said to me, 'you can fill your head with facts and it won't make any difference unless you know Jesus. He *is* the answer. Now I know you probably don't believe that. You may think I'm some sort of lunatic. They always make us out to be lunatics in the news these days. And yet, ask yourself this: who controls the news? The atheists. The liberals. No offense, but how can you trust the story if the storyteller is motivated to twist the truth?'

'Don't preach, Neville!'

'And speaking of the news, you must have heard the story about Sir Kenneth and that student of his? An illicit involvement, they're saying. An abortion!'

'Yes, I've heard the news.'

'We will *not* judge them,' the woman said sternly, flashing a glance over the frames of her glasses.

'Why can't we judge them? Wrong is wrong.'

'Neville.'

'And I was only going to make a point about the media, Mother. When a Christian does something wrong, it's proof of the evils of Christianity, but when anybody else does wrong, it's because of human frailty. That's how the media spins it. I stand by my word. Jesus is the answer.'

'I see,' I said. 'And what is the question?'

'Huh?'

'If he's the answer then there must be a question.'

'*That* is a good one,' the woman laughed.

'The question is *Why?*' Neville said after a moment's thought. 'Why anything? Why are you here? Why am I here? Why do things happen the way they do? If you can't answer those questions, or if you answer them wrongly, then everything goes amiss. Everything!'

He is a fool, I thought. But he is right.

'Here, take this,' Neville said, handing me a pamphlet entitled *Reasons to Believe*. 'This will explain everything.'

'That's unnecessary. I'm a practicing Anglican.'

'What? But I thought you said you were from the conference?'

'I am from the conference.'

'Then what are you doing there?'

'I am listening, mostly.'

'Listening to what?'

'Just listening.'

Neville's eyes narrowed, regarding me curiously now, as if I had transformed into something unrecognizable.

'Why are you so surprised, my dear?' the woman said. 'In the body of Christ, some people are the ears. And we need more ears. We have so many mouths, after all.'

I exchanged a smile with the woman and excused myself. I began wandering through the thin crowd in search of the Munichs. As I rounded the hill a young woman looked over from the edge of the grass. It was the milk maid. She was with another young woman. A newspaper was spread open between them, pinned down with drink bottles and wrapped sandwiches.

She recognized me and smiled. It was the same chaste smile that she gave to me and to every guest without fail—the kind of smile that welcomed you but did not overstep its bounds.

I nodded and continued around the hill. Swallows soared over a nearby meadow, yipping as they wheeled. I finished the circuit of the hill and reached the road.

I headed into the centre of the village next, where I wandered about for a while, keeping an eye out for the family. The village had a population of only about three thousand but contained everything you might find in a town: hotels and restaurants and cafés, businesses and stores and boutiques, a grocery with underground parking, an indoor arena, a three-screen cinema. It was remarkably peaceful, neatly laid out around a stream along with numerous picturesque chalets, surrounded by lush meadows and the sprawling glory of the mountains.

The village church clanged three o'clock. I had a coffee and almond croissant at the bakery, and watched Wimbledon on an overhead screen. The Swiss favourite was playing in his opening match, finishing off his first victim. My phone was on the table and I kept glancing at it, hoping for a reply from Delia.

It seemed obvious, a cliché, that I was attracted to her because we were opposites. I wondered if she felt the same way? We offered what the other lacked: through me, she might get closer to a God she could never believe in, and through her, I might get farther away from a God who'd become harder to believe in.

The Swiss struck a blazing forehand. His opponent, a lanky Croatian, flicked it back and clipped the net cord. A lucky shot.

My phone buzzed, flashing to life.

It was only a text message from Flange: *Going for a hike on the big waterfall alp. Want to come? At the bus station in 10 minutes.*

I wrote back: *Did you find Delia?*

The reply came quickly: *No sign of her yet. Inspector S was here and wants to speak to her.*

SIXTEEN

THE VILLAGE BUS terminal was a short walk from the bakery. A yellow postal bus had just arrived from Frutigen and passengers were unloading packs and suitcases from a luggage trailer. I found the sign for the Alpkäppli and it wasn't long before people from the conference began trickling into the station, forming a small crowd on the platform.

Flange wore a canvas backpack but was otherwise dressed in his usual ruffled suit jacket, tan trousers, and brown loafers, as if heading off to a lecture at Harvard.

'I didn't realize you'd left the hotel,' he said.

'I went out for a walk. What's going on with the conference? Don't the sessions go till five?'

'We decided to cancel the symposium on sexual morality. Didn't seem fitting under the circumstances. Anyway, we came up with plan B, which was to reschedule the mountain hike for today instead of tomorrow. Nothing like a change of scenery to distract people from a scandal. I hope you weren't searching for Delia?'

'I was at the bakery watching Wimbledon.'

He eyed me doubtfully. 'Resist the temptation, my friend. You've been warned.'

'You said the Inspector was looking for her?'

'Oh yes, he showed up with his little notepad. He said to let him know if anyone learned of her whereabouts. It's the talk of the conference. I assume she's hiding out in the village somewhere. They would have picked her up if she tried to get out—unless she hiked over one of the mountains.'

'The police have her under some kind of suspicion, then?'

'I'm sure it's just protocol, like the first time they came around. Leo's in a foul mood about the whole thing,' he said in a low voice, glancing back at Granger. 'The rumours are really flying—and some of them are unfortunately morbid.'

'You mean people are wondering if she was involved in his death.'

'It's such utter nonsense! Delia Stoltz may be manipulative but she isn't a murderer. By the way, I saw Blakey and he told me about your conversation. Your questions about that watch.'

'They were just questions.'

'It doesn't help the situation for you to be poking about. Leo would be more than a little peeved to find out you were playing detective.'

'He seems to dislike me.'

'Don't worry, he dislikes most people. As for this Delia business, it's getting out of hand. She may have slept with Ken, but she obviously didn't murder him. Nobody murdered him. People are connecting dots that shouldn't be connected.'

'Has Eleanor heard the news yet?'

'Leo called her a little while ago. He didn't get into the details with me, but I imagine she took it badly. She and Ken were married over forty years. It's a sad ending. I mean, if you're going to die on your wife, it's best not to do it while you've been sleeping with another woman.'

I nodded, thinking of my own mother after my father's death. She'd mostly hidden her suffering behind a stony face. She still refused to talk about him. I didn't blame her.

The bus rumbled into the station. We boarded, showing our hotel passes, and squeezed into the back, where Flange fell into conversation with Granger and a professor from Edinburgh. The bus lumbered down the main road and after several sharp turns continued down the valley, following a shallow bluish stream that rushed over a rocky riverbed. Now and then I glimpsed the great waterfall that plunged down the mountain in a heap of white mist.

It took fifteen minutes to reach the gondola base station. The cable car held only twenty-five passengers at a time and Flange and I managed to slip in with the first group. As the car rose, I spotted a narrow path that climbed the slope in a zigzag pattern. Cows were filing up, clambering through the mud, dangerously close to the edge, led by a man with a cane. Behind me, between the faces of the other passengers, the village receded and shrunk into the vastness of the valley where the chalets were sprinkled like toys over patches of green meadow; and on the furthest edge of the village I spotted the white flash of the Pfannli.

The top of the alp was several hundred metres above the valley. A brown cow was grazing placidly outside the station exit. The air was cooler but not cold; the sky was clear and I could feel its warmth over my face, and the smell of mud and manure wafted in the air.

The alp was an oval pasture one kilometer by two kilometres wide, encircled by the Alpkäppli and several other ridges. The mountain glistened with snow, and veins of snow ran down its ravines and thinned and melted into the gravel slope and the grassy plain, which was strewn with large boulders and criss-crossed with streams that joined together and led to the precipice, where the great falls tumbled into the valley. Cows were grazing here and there, and a cluster of goats ambled toward us, bells jingling.

'That looks like a restaurant,' I said to Flange, pointing out a rustic chalet with a patio and tables.

'Of course,' he chuckled. 'What's the use of climbing a Swiss mountain if you can't have fondue when you get to the top?'

We meandered along the plain with others from the

conference, following pathways and tracking through swaths of wet grass. We circled around cows and stepped over dung heaps, and the closer we got to the Alpkäppli the more streams we encountered. They snaked through the green, and the ground became softer and lumpier and wetter, so that we had to leap from boulders to dry spots, and from dry spots to boulders, until at last we reached the lower slopes of the mountain.

We collected clumps of brown snow and hurled them at each other. It was great amusement, and even Leo Granger was laughing, and the troubles of the village seemed to fade away.

We filed back across the plain tired and hungry. There was talk about going to the restaurant, and a few people headed that way. I had some fresh bread in my pack that I'd picked up at the bakery, and Flange had a little bread too, and some cheese, prosciutto, and a small bottle of French wine. We shared our morsels as we walked, and talked about our plans for the future. Flange would be defending his thesis in a few months and hoped to land a job at a university, while I expected to take a more clinical route and work with therapy patients.

'I'm surprised that you want to be a psychotherapist,' he said.

'Why's that?'

He took a swig of wine. 'I don't mean to be presumptuous, but you really should reconsider. Working with depressed people will just bore you, or turn you into one of them. You'd have more freedom as an academic. You get to go to places like this, all expenses paid for.'

'It is quite beautiful here.'

'Aren't you glad you came? Now be honest with me, Conner. In this moment, surrounded by the natural magnificence of these mountains, breathing the fresh air and gulping cheap wine, what need do you have of God? Don't think about it, just tell me, what need?'

Before I could respond, a voice said, 'Vee haff need of Gott, wezzer we say so or no.'

We turned and beheld the preacher; it was the fellow we had seen yesterday—the young man with the long hair. He had a moustache too, a little one like a postage stamp, so that he looked like a cross between Hitler and a hippie. A small group of men and women were walking with him.

'I don't recall inviting you into this conversation,' Flange said.

'I speak za druth.'

'And what is the basis of your truth? What evidence do you have that there is a God, and that we have any need of this God?'

'Vee haff za verd of za Lord.'

'The word of the Lord? You must mean the Bible, that old collection of fables. Suppose I put together my own collection of stories and declared it was the truth? How could you determine whether your collection of stories was a better representation of truth than my collection of stories?'

'Can your shtories zave a man's zol?'

'No, because man does not have a soul. But my stories, if well written, might uplift his emotions, or impart some useful wisdom to his brain. That might be a worthy accomplishment.'

There were murmurs of protest in the Preacher's group. A young woman who could not have been more than eighteen declared that Flange was 'close-minded'. Flange gave a disdainful laugh and replied that his mind was only closed to nonsense. He and the group continued trading remarks for a couple of minutes, until the path joined up with a larger path, where Leo Granger and others from the conference happened to be walking. They overheard the exchange and immediately joined in.

'Yu peeple av no objictive pruf of Gaud!' shouted the professor from Edinburgh in the surliest of Scottish accents.

'But you can't prove there *isn't* a God!' insisted the young woman.

'Absurrrd! Tha onus is on *yu* ta pruf tha something *is* tha case, noh fah *mee* to pruf tha tit's *noh* tha case!'

'I don't need to prove it,' the woman declared. 'Because I know it.'

'*Hauw* do yu know?'

'I know with my knower,' she said, patting her heart.

'So God is a feeling?' Granger said. 'What kind of proof is that?'

'Do you not zee zat Gott iz all around us?' the Preacher said, looking up and about. 'Do you not zee in za mountains? Do you sink all zis iz only an accident?'

'Yes, yes!' the atheists shouted. 'It's an accident!'

'And a beautiful accident!' Flange cried. He clambered onto a large lichen-stained boulder and shook his wine bottle. 'Chance is beautiful, chance is beautiful!'

The atheists took up the words, chanting it together and laughing.

A man with a ruddy face climbed onto another boulder nearby. 'Listen!' he called out. 'Everybody listen! I was trained as a scientist, and the pastor here is correct. Life is no accident. It couldn't have happened by chance. Do you realize that the odds of forming even a very basic form of life, such as a simple protein, is one in ten to the power of three hundred and ninety! Do you know how small that probability is? Now just imagine how unlikely it is for something as complex as human life to develop. It's like a tornado touching down in a junkyard and assembling a Boeing 747! It's impossible without divine intervention!'

Cheers and denunciations erupted from the mixed crowd. 'Yu'v misunderstud tha facts!' called out the professor from Edinburgh. 'Tha development of life was *noh* instantaneous, boota incremental process tha startid with simple chemicals tha transmuted into polymers, replicating polymers, hypercycles, bacteria—'

'You are missing za big pikchah!' the Preacher cried out. He had climbed up the boulder beside the ruddy-faced man. 'Gott iz bigger zan za little details!'

'No he isn't!' bellowed Granger, pulling himself up

beside Flange. 'Because there is no such thing as God. Everything we see around us can be explained through natural mechanisms. The only reason people still cling to God is because they are afraid. It's the only reason they've ever believed. Fear is at the heart of all religious belief.'

'Our fear iz a fear of reverenz!' said the Preacher. 'Za Psalmist said—'

'Your reverence is a euphemism for terror!' Granger shot back. 'You are afraid of death, you are afraid of suffering, you are afraid of sickness—that is why you believe! Religion is a crutch! God is a security blanket! If we could build a society that was safe, and a world in which there were homes, jobs, and education for all, nobody would need a God. Why do you think belief in God has dwindled in the West? Because we have medicine! Because we have food supplies! Because we have peace and knowledge!'

'No,' the Preacher replied, 'because vee are proud, zelfish, materialistic, and greedy. Vee don't vant Gott because he vood challenge our pride, he vood challenge our materialism and zelfishness—and vee don't vant to give zose tings up. Zat iz vhy vee reject Gott. Vee reject Gott because vee vant to be our own gotts!'

'I'd rather be my own God than be controlled by the church—or the likes of *you*!' Flange said. 'I would rather face the challenges of life honestly rather than clinging to a lie!'

More cheers and boos. I was taking pictures with my phone. The ruddy-faced man piped up: 'Without God, we cannot truly know the difference between good and evil, between right and wrong. Without God, our morality is determined by our feelings. Look at your beloved Sir Kenneth Chatwin. You read the newspapers today, didn't you? He had an affair with his student! What kind of morality is that? On what basis did he conclude that it was right to sleep with her? On what basis did he conclude that it was right to impregnate her?'

'How dare you!' Flange shouted.

'Who made *yu* judge over peeple's chaices?' added the professor from Edinburgh.

'Did he have any regard for his wife when he had sex with that girl?' the ruddy-faced man went on. 'And when that girl had an abortion, did he have any regard for the life that was snuffed out?'

'It was just an embryo!' somebody shouted.

'A cluster of cells!' somebody cried.

The Preacher thrust his finger ominously at Flange and Granger: 'Vizout Gott, vee are lost! Vee are filled vith all unrighteousness, zexual immorality, vickedness, covetousness, maliciousness, full of envy, and murder! Yes, even murder! Murder!'

SEVENTEEN

WITH A SAVAGE cry Flange hurled the wine bottle at him. The Preacher saw it coming and ducked at the last moment, but managed to keep his finger up while still shouting *Murder, Murder!* All the more enraged, Flange leaped off the boulder and pushed through the crowd and grabbed the Preacher's pant leg, pulling him down.

The Preacher tumbled to the ground. Flange got onto his back, straddling him, and started shaking him by the collar, slapping his face into the sopping grass. A moment later someone tackled Flange, while everybody else began shouting and shoving.

'Stop, you idiots!' Granger shouted. 'They're filming! Stop!'

I wasn't the only one. Several people were standing on the margins with their phones and tablets aimed at the scene. The realization spread quickly among the combatants, who began glancing about self-consciously.

The scuffling dwindled. Silence fell. The Preacher sat

up, panting, and brushed the dripping stands of hair from his face.

'Gott punishes zinners!' he cried. 'You vill zee!'

'Oh go to hell,' someone replied.

There was a burst of laughter. The two groups began dissolving. I helped Flange up and we wandered back to the main path with Granger and the professor from Edinburgh. People clapped Flange on the shoulder and congratulated him. He smiled weakly. There was a scrape on his forehead.

'You sure you're okay?' Granger said.

'I'm fine.'

'You shouldn't have lost control.'

'You heard what they said.'

'We're better than they are, Jeremy. We need to show it.'

With that, Granger gave me a moody glance. He and the professor walked together while Flange and I trailed behind.

'Of course I lost control,' Flange said quietly. 'They made it personal. You heard what they said about Ken and Delia.'

'It was personal even before they said those things.'

'They went too far.'

'Everybody went too far.'

'They attacked his character, Conner. They accused him and Delia of killing a so-called *life*. A bunch of cells the size of a poppy seed! Are you saying that doesn't justify some kind of response?'

'Emotions are high, Flange.'

'You think I have no right to be angry?'

'That's not what I said.'

'Or let me guess—you think abortion is murder? You actually agree with them, right?'

'I'm saying it's not a good time to talk about it.'

'Maybe it's a good time to stop talking altogether.'

He walked ahead of me.

'Flange, come on.'

He kept walking. I decided it was best to let him cool off.

Everybody was heading back to the gondola station. It was almost seven o'clock and the sun had disappeared behind the Alpkäppli, although its light was still visible, a bright golden band across the surrounding peaks. I was tired, having walked more than expected today, and was dismayed to find that the doors were closed when I reached the gondola station.

A small wrinkled woman from the restaurant was on a bench with a handful of brochures. She explained that the last cable car had departed for the day. A few rental rooms were available above the restaurant. Apart from that, the only option was to take the cow path down the mountain.

I decided on the latter, as did everybody else. It was the same zigzagging path that I had seen on the ride up to the alp. We proceeded in a single straggling line, atheists and Christians, trudging down the dark green slope like weary soldiers. The path was pocked with hoof prints and smeared with heaps of dung. We could not see the waterfall, although the roar of it was constant, and now and then we felt its mist in the air.

My phone buzzed. I took it out of my pocket.

A message from Delia.

Can I trust you?

Heart pounding, I halted and looked up, gazing over the treetops toward the valley. Flange was right: she was probably still down there somewhere.

As much as I wanted to respond to her, I slipped the phone away. I didn't want to act on impulse. I needed time to think.

The path descended into a sun-mottled wood. Slugs crept along the ground, tentacles probing. I spotted an ibex on the other side of a ravine; it was poised on a rock, its horns like a pair of curved swords. The sound of rushing water grew louder and the path led along a precipice that offered a stunning view of the waterfall.

I paused with the other walkers to take in the sight. The falls spilled down in long white threads, smashing over a rugged cascade of rocks to a pool.

Everybody murmured in quiet wonder. I thought of Sir Kenneth; I thought of him lying under the Pfannli with his face down; and behind his body, like a dim shadow, was the memory of my father.

I had come to terms with his death, but I'd never gotten over his affair. It still hurt, that betrayal.

I actually knew the woman he had been involved with. I'd met her many years before the two of them died in the cottage. She was a school teacher, a single mother, who had lived in our neighbourhood for a brief time. I'd played street hockey with her son, a timid, distracted boy who was often ridiculed for allowing too many goals in net.

That winter the boy and his mother came to our house on several occasions for supper. I don't know what triggered the invitations. Maybe my mother felt sorry that the woman was alone. I was six or seven years old, and my only recollection of these encounters was playing cars with the boy while my parents and the woman sat around the coffee table. Was it then, during those casual conversations, that she and my father felt the spark of attraction? Those first cautious glances must have seemed innocent.

There was no sign of an affair that winter, or at any point, until she and my father were found in the cottage bedroom. I saw the room once. The bed was a four-poster, high off the floor, with fat red pillows. By the time the paramedics arrived the bodies would have been stiff; locked in a frozen embrace, like two statues. Did they have to break their limbs to extricate them from each other? I shuddered at the thought.

Disturbingly, nobody seemed to know how long they had been involved with each other. Had they recently met again and developed a relationship? Had it been going on for a decade, since those winter meals and cups of tea? There were no letters, no clues, nothing. The affair might have been a one-time lapse in judgement, or my entire childhood might have been lived out in the shadow of a well-managed lie.

Either way, it hurt. I felt bitter. If there was any good that came out of it, it was that I swore I'd never make my father's mistake. I don't just mean the mistake of having an affair. I mean the mistake of making a decision without counting the cost to the people around me.

My father had ignored that cost. So had Sir Kenneth, for that matter. This was no moral judgement, just a psychological fact: selfishness, like a stone, plunges gladly into its own little pool of needs, rarely giving attention to the ripple effects.

I moved away from the precipice and walked on. The path curved and descended into the trees, and at last began to level out.

We reached the foot of the mountain. The bus was idling at the base station. I made an exhausted dash to reach it, along with several others, before the doors closed.

Glancing over my shoulder, I spotted Flange in the rear of the vehicle. He was leaning back with his eyes closed. I thought of responding to Delia, and almost reached for my phone, but again resisted. I shouldn't have sent her that text message earlier. There was nothing I could do to help her. It would be a mistake to get any closer. We weren't right for each other. Hadn't I decided that a few hours ago?

I went back and forth on the matter, struggling with myself, until the bus rounded a bend in the village and I spotted the Munich family. They were ambling up a lane, each of them laden with a yellow and green backpack.

'Stop the bus,' I told the driver.

'I cannot stop before the stop.'

'Please, I need to get off here.'

'I am sorry, I cannot.'

I gave an outraged gasp, which he politely ignored. A minute later we reached the next stop and I dashed out of the bus and ran up a road. It curved and forked and I veered to the left, following a path to a series of steps, and as I reached the top I spotted the Munichs ahead. They'd paused at a construction barrier, peering into a trench beside a shop.

They turned and stared as I ran up. 'Good evening,' I said, panting. 'Pardon the interruption. I need to speak with you about something.'

The girl drifted closer to her mother. The boy watched me sullenly, his front tooth dangling over his bottom lip.

I produced the watch. 'Have you seen this before?'

'Das ist ja meine Uhr, Mama!' the girl cried.

'So you recognize it?' I said, guessing at her words. 'Did he take it from you? Was it on your doll when your brother ran away with it?'

'How do you know these things?' Frau Munich said. 'Where did you find that?'

'I found it outside the hotel.'

'Outside?'

'But there's some question about how it got there,

which is what I wanted to ask you about. I was told that your son ran away with his sister's doll and that you followed him to the billiards area, looking for the doll and a heart watch. That was on Sunday night. He had hidden the doll in the tree, but he told you that he didn't have the watch. Do you remember?'

'How do you know this?'

'Some men were playing billiards at the time. One of them told me what happened. I need to know whether your son had the watch with him. I realize this is a strange question, but it's quite important. What did he do with this watch? It was around the doll's neck and I believe that he snapped it off—you can see the chain is broken. But what did he do with it then?'

Herr Munich, whose English was limited, turned to his wife. She started speaking to him in German, evidently explaining what I'd said. Then she looked down at the boy and addressed him. *Klaus*, she called him.

Klaus' eyes darted away, his tongue flicking nervously at the rogue tooth.

Frau Munich sighed and looked at her husband. The man took the boy's arm and spoke firmly. A threat was being issued. The boy stopped flicking. He glanced at me and began to speak.

'He says he pulled the watch from the doll,' Frau Munich said, translating. 'He says he hid it in a jacket on the couch.'

'A jacket on the couch? What jacket?'

'Why do you ask these things? Who are you?'

‘My name is Conner. I’m from the conference. Look, it’s rather urgent. I realize this is unexpected, and I promise that I will explain everything—eventually. I only need to know about the jacket? Whose was it?’

Frau Munich watched me. The thin skin on her bony face was reddened, burned over the nose. The family must have been hiking all afternoon. She began questioning the boy again, and then she looked at me and said: ‘He only says there was a jacket on the couch beside the billiards table. He put it in a pocket so I would not find it.’

I recalled Blakey’s description of the scene: the boy was hidden behind the couch. The jacket must have been draped over it, the pocket hanging before him.

‘Does he remember anything at all about the jacket?’ I said. ‘The colour or the fabric?’

The mother asked him. The boy shook his head.

‘He does not know,’ she said. ‘Will you give us the watch now? It was a gift to my daughter.’

‘A gift?’

‘Yes. From a young woman at the hotel.’

‘What woman?’

‘She is with your group. The woman who was eating with you in the *Speisesaal*. The one with the red hair.’

EIGHTEEN

I RAN OFF. 'I'm sorry!' I called over my shoulder. 'I'll return the watch soon!'

The Munichs shouted after me, and I heard the girl wailing 'Mama!', but I kept running, up the lane and around a corner, and only stopped when I'd reached the main road.

I phoned Delia. She answered immediately. 'Conner?'

'In response to your question—yes, you can trust me.'

I halted and looked back.

'Where are you?' she said.

'I'm in the village.'

'Where?'

'The main road.'

'Where exactly?'

I looked about. 'Beside the Hotel Xavier. The place with the tennis courts. Are you still here?'

'Look down the road. What do you see?'

'I see some shops. And the village church.'

'There. You found me.'

I hurried down the road and crossed to the other side. The church grounds were raised above the road, with the building itself set back, so that I could only see the upper part of the walls and the old stone clock tower with its golden numerals.

I climbed the stone steps and passed under an arched gate. The grassy grounds were well-groomed and planted with flowerbeds. Delia was sitting in the shadows of the portico smoking a cigarette.

'What are you doing here?' I said.

'It's a peaceful place,' she said. 'If you don't mind the company of angels and devils.'

She was referring to the fresco behind her. It was old and faded by the weather, but the main scene was clear. The Last Judgement. Christ was seated on his throne flanked by Mary and the apostles. Underneath were the damned enduring various tortures in hell. A man's tongue was being torn out with pliers. Children were packed into a boiling cauldron, sunken up to their chins, while a demon pumped at the bellows, fanning the flames.

'How long have you been here?' I said.

'Most of the day. I figured nobody would look for me in a church.'

I had a hand in my pocket, meaning to show her the watch; then I changed my mind, deciding to see how much she'd reveal on her own. 'You never told me about you and Sir Kenneth,' I said.

'Do you really think I would share that with you in our first conversation?'

'So it's true, what they're saying?'

She expelled a stream of smoke. 'It's all true. We had a relationship. I got pregnant. He asked me to get rid of it and...so I did. And then he ended it with me.'

She stared toward the churchyard.

'Do you have any idea who leaked the story?' I said.

She shook her head. She took another drag on the cigarette and flicked it away. 'They say that before this church was built, it snowed on the meadow here, and the snow fell in the shape of a cross. Do you believe that? Do you believe that God could choose a place, and make a symbol on the ground?'

'I believe it's possible.'

'What about this fresco behind me? Do you see the heads of the babies in the cauldron? They're burning in hell because they weren't baptized. Do you believe that's possible too?'

'I don't believe everything the church has ever taught.'

'What do you believe, then?'

'I only have pieces of the truth, Delia. I don't have everything.'

'We agree on something, then. Life is uncertain.' She wiped her eyes. 'I don't want to stay out here. I'm not ready to face anybody else.'

I followed her into the church. The door was heavy, and it was dim and cool inside, smelling of wood. The ceiling was arched, held up by hewn beams and pillars. There was no sound but the shuffle of our footsteps on the stone floor.

Verses were inscribed on the walls in Gothic letters. I recognized one: Psalm 119, verse 9. *How can a young man keep his way pure? By guarding it according to Your word.*

'Will you tell me what happened, Delia?'

'I already told you what happened.'

'I mean, how did it begin?'

'How do you think it began? I fell in love.'

'You fell in love with Sir Kenneth?'

She walked up the aisle, as far as the altar. 'I was already an atheist before I knew Ken. But there was one question I wasn't able to answer until he came into my life.'

'What question?'

'If life evolved by chance,' she said, turning toward me, 'then how can it have any meaning? That may not seem like much to you, since you probably have your own answer, but it nagged at me. Sometimes it filled me with despair. If the universe is just an accident then what is the purpose of my existence? What is the purpose of anyone's? What does it matter how we live, whether selfishly, or compassionately, when the universe itself doesn't care? In the eyes of a meaningless universe, Mother Theresa is no better than Adolf Hitler. Shakespeare is no more poetic than the shrieking of a monkey.'

'And Sir Kenneth gave you an answer?'

'When I was in undergrad I read *The Probabilities of Life*. There wasn't anything new in that book, nothing that hadn't been said before, but it was the way that Ken said it. The way he put it all together. It clicked suddenly. I could believe in a godless universe without being nihilistic. I could believe in a godless universe and still have beauty, and meaning, and purpose—and even morality. It was liberating. He gave me the strength to believe.'

'To believe in what?'

'In nothing. And everything.'

She sat in the front pew. I walked up and sat beside her. Behind the altar were three windows stained with blue and red and green and purple; but the light was so dim, and the glass so blackened, that I could not make out the figures depicted in the scenes.

'I applied to Mount Albert for graduate school because Ken was there,' she said. 'He seemed enthusiastic to take me on—me and Blakey. Ken's judgement wasn't perfect when it came to students. Blakey is an imbecile. And a drunk.'

'I understand he's sober now.'

She looked at me.

'Flange mentioned it.'

'Flange. I can only imagine what he's saying about me.'

'He was surprised at the news. He said the police want to speak with you.'

'I know. The Inspector left a message on my phone. Maybe he thinks I killed Ken? Me, the jilted lover. It makes a good story, doesn't it?'

'If you have nothing to hide, then why are you hiding out here?'

'Because my life is falling apart. And I didn't just come here to hide. I came here for help. To pray to the God I don't believe in.'

'You prayed?'

'Well, I talked to my own ego. Does that count?' She gave a small laugh that faded into the shadows. 'I would have replied to your message sooner, but I was afraid. I thought you would judge me.'

'I only want to understand how all of this happened. How you got involved and how things got to where they are.'

'Do you want to know this because you're interested in me, or because you're suspicious about why he died?'

'I don't think that you killed him, Delia.'

'Well that's a relief.'

'But I am suspicious about his death.'

'So you want to know all about my personal life, but you don't really care about me? You're just solving a puzzle?'

'I didn't say that.'

'Then what are you saying? Do I matter in any of this? I'm just wondering.'

'I go slowly when it comes to feelings.'

'Why, are you afraid?'

'Disciplined. I've learned some lessons.'

She was quiet for a few moments. I could hear the faint chirping of the birds outside.

'For the longest time Ken treated me like any other student,' she said. 'It was painful, because I felt so much for him. Here was the man I could have spent my life with, if only I had been born into a different time, or a different circumstance. But I wondered if it might still be possible.'

'To have a relationship with him?'

'Yes.'

'Even though he was married? Even though he was two-and-a-half times your age?'

'*Now* you're judging me.'

'I'm asking rational questions. There were risks to your being involved with him. People could get hurt. His wife, for instance.'

'Eleanor, the old battle-axe?'

'Are you saying her feelings don't count?'

'Look, it wasn't a rational thing with Ken. I was head over heels. I wasn't trying to hurt anyone. I was in love, and it just happened to be with him. I've always tended to fall for intelligent men. I slept with my high school science teacher because it was a joy to hear him talk. Have you ever been turned on by somebody talking about the anatomy of a blood cell?'

'I can't say I have.'

'People fall in love for different reasons. For me, talking with Ken was an intimate thing. Abstract conversation felt somehow...erotic. You must think I'm strange?'

'You make me nervous about speaking with you.'

'Don't worry. You're bright but you're not Ken. I think I can control myself.'

I felt a stab of hurt; I smiled to cover it.

There was a ping and she took out her phone. 'A text from Jeremy. *Are you alive or what?* Such a sensitive way to ask. The jerk.'

She turned the phone off.

'Anyway,' she went on. 'So I had these feelings for Ken, and then the stroke happened. That was last June. It was pretty bad during the first few weeks. He was half paralyzed and could barely speak. He had staring spells when he seemed to blank out. Nobody knew whether he was going to get better. And then he did. Slowly. It was like a miracle. By the end of the year he was back at work. Everything seemed to be getting back to normal. That's all I wanted. The old Ken. Then I went to see him one day about a research project.'

'When was that?'

'A few months ago. March nineteenth. It was late in the day and we ended up talking for a while. When I was about to leave his office he got up and walked me to the door, and I looked at him, and we kissed. It was one of those moments that you can never remember, although in retrospect you see that your entire life was headed for it. The moment that changed everything. It started from there—not that it lasted long,' she said glumly.

‘When did it end?’

‘About a month ago. It was his decision. I had some trouble accepting it.’

‘Is that why you took a room next to him in the hotel?’

‘Yes. He asked me to change rooms but I refused. I wanted to show him that he couldn’t just push me away. We had quite a row on Saturday morning. It was the day after I arrived. Eleanor had left the hotel by then. I think he might have told her something—or maybe everything. He said he couldn’t be my supervisor anymore. He said that after the conference I should find somebody else to work with. I felt so betrayed. He’d promised me all sorts of things when we were together.’

‘Promised you what?’

‘Oh, the usual little lies that men tell women. Big lies, actually. He’d leave Eleanor, he said. We’d do research together and write books and travel. He wanted to be the father of my baby. That was his idea, you know. I never wanted a baby before then, but I went along with it. I knew he might not have long to live. He was at risk for another stroke, could end up in a wheelchair. I knew all this and I was willing to take that chance because I actually believed we might have a few good years together. I was such an idiot! Of course he changed his mind a few weeks after I got pregnant. That’s when the reality began to sink in. He decided, then, that everything we’d talked about was just a fantasy. He couldn’t go through with it. It would destroy Eleanor, ruin his reputation, bring down the whole edifice—those were his words, *bring down the whole edifice!* As if his life was so grand and precious compared to mine! We fought about it for days. I tried to persuade him to keep the baby, but that only infuriated him. He threatened to cut me off if I didn't...'

'If you didn't get rid of it?'

'Yes.'

'And if you did?'

'If I did, we could continue our relationship in secret. But it turns out that was just another promise.'

I waited, staring at the arched windows behind the altar.

'I did what he wanted,' she said. 'I'm no feminist when it comes to this. I believe in biology not rhetoric. By five weeks there's a beating heart. If wombs had windows nobody would get an abortion.'

She pressed her face into her hands.

I put my arm around her. She leaned closer and wept and I stared at the windows. My vision had adjusted to the low light and I could make out the scene in the glass. It was a garden. Jesus was on his knees, looking up at a blood-red sky, and the disciples had fallen asleep around him.

NINETEEN

I CONVINCED HER to go back to the hotel. She agreed to call Inspector Black Dove in the morning. We left the church and started down the main road. It was almost nine o'clock but there was still light in the sky.

I took out my phone.

'Are you going to ignore me now?' she said.

'I'm looking for something on the Internet. There was an incident this afternoon on the Alpkäppli—the mountain with the big waterfall. People were filming with their phones, and I suspect the video may have been uploaded.'

'What video? What happened?'

'There was a debate between some people from the conference and the fundamentalists. There were references to you and Sir Kenneth.'

'References?'

'To the abortion.'

'Those bastards. What did they say?'

We paused under a shop awning and I briefly recounted the incident. I could see the pain in her face but I knew it was best to tell her; she'd hear about it one way or another. Then, after a couple minutes of searching on my phone, I found a video just as I'd expected, among some recently uploaded clips. It was cleverly titled *Battle of the Alps: Atheists versus Christians.*

'I was right,' I said. 'It's here. Are you sure you want to watch this?'

'Play it.'

The clip started with the Preacher. He was on top of the boulder, declaring that God was bigger than the 'little details'. Granger's voice boomed out and the camera swung toward him, and then it panned back and forth as the debate unfolded. The images were shaky but the audio was clear.

I noticed the counter at the bottom of the video. There were already more than a thousand views. It was going viral.

Murder! the Preacher shouted. *Murder!*

Delia sighed.

'We should stop it,' I said.

'No.'

Flange threw the wine bottle. He attacked. I hadn't seen his expression until now; I had been standing behind him during the actual event. His face was twisted with fury as he straddled the Preacher's back, slamming the man's face into the wet grass. I had never seen Flange so enraged.

'That's it,' I said as the clip ended. I put the phone away. 'I'm sorry you had to see that.'

We started walking again. A ripe orange glow lay on the upper slopes of the Grüneggli ridge.

'I'm leaving tomorrow,' she said. 'I'll talk to the police and then I'm leaving. I'm finished with the conference.'

'I understand.'

'Why don't you come with me?'

'Come where?'

'I don't know. We can see the sights. You have a few days left in the country, don't you?'

'I've got a talk scheduled for Thursday. I shouldn't just walk out.'

'Fine,' she said indifferently.

A Vespa sputtered past and the Hotel Iselin came into view between the chalets along the road. The grassy hill on the other side of the road was empty.

We entered the hotel through a lower entrance by the parking lot. A corridor led us to the stairwell and we climbed to the second floor. 'Do you want to come in?' she said as we reached her room.

'Alright. But I can only stay for a few minutes. I need to talk to Flange.'

'What for?'

'He was a bit upset after what happened on the alp.'

'At least he stood up for me. Not that I deserved it.'

She unlocked the door and opened it and I noticed two things. The first was that the balcony door was open. The second was a male figure in a suit jacket, kneeling over an open suitcase on the floor.

'Flange?' I said. 'What are you doing here?'

'How dare you!' Delia cried. 'How dare you!'

She ran at him and he shielded his head while she began pummeling him with her fists. He ran out of the room and she chased him into the corridor.

I went to the door and peered out. She had pursued him into the stairwell. I went back inside and noticed the dresser drawers were open. They were bare. I looked at the suitcase. A pair of green underwear was draped over it.

Averting my eyes, I noticed a book on the floor amid some other items of clothing. It was *The Probabilities of Life*. A postcard was sticking out of it. It was from Budapest, showing a photo of the ornate parliament building.

I pulled out the card and flipped it over. The writing was messy but I could make out a few fragments: *My dearest...so beautiful here...miss you...gypsy market...will bring something back for you.*

It was signed KC.

As I tucked the postcard back into the book, I noticed a folded paper within the pages—a sheet of blue-rimmed hotel stationery. I slipped it out and unfolded it. A few sentences had been scrawled on the page in the same messy script as on the postcard: *when the words... we...I...rain.*

I heard the door open and turned. Delia crossed the floor and snapped the page out of my hands.

'Get out of here!' she said. 'Get out!'

I started toward the door.

'Wait,' she said. 'Don't go.'

I stood and waited. She began gathering the scattered clothes into the suitcase. 'I can't believe that bastard got in here.'

'What do you think he was doing?'

'What kind of question is that? Probably sniffing my underwear. The pervert.'

'Did you catch up to him?'

'No.'

'Why were all your clothes in a suitcase?'

'I started packing this morning after I saw the news. It was a little while after we talked. I was going to leave the village and then changed my mind. I wasn't sure what to do. That's when I went to hide.'

'You left your balcony door unlocked.'

'Are you blaming *me* that he got in?'

'I'm simply pointing out—'

'Why would I lock it? I'm on the second floor.'

'Of course.'

I went outside and peered around the barrier that separated Delia's balcony from the one on the left. Flange's balcony was the next one over. 'He had to have climbed across your neighbour's balcony to get here,' I called back.

She came out and looked. 'He's probably the one who spread the news about me.'

'Why would you think that?'

'Last month I had a problem with my computer. I took it to a guy for repair and he discovered a virus on it—a virus that would allow somebody to access everything on my machine. My email, my pictures, everything.'

'But earlier you said you didn't know how the story got out.'

'I knew *how* it got out. What you asked in the church was *who* had leaked it. Anyway, do I need to give you every detail about myself? I spill out my whole personal life and you treat me like something under a microscope.'

'I'm only trying to understand things.'

'Right.' She went back into the room in a huff.

I followed her. 'That paper I was looking at,' I said. 'It was on Hotel Iselin stationery. I was wondering—'

'God, are you going to interrogate me all evening? Can't we talk about something else?'

'I don't mean to pry, but it's rather important.'

'Alright. What.'

'That paper—I couldn't make out all the words but they said something about *words* and *rain*. What was it?'

'It was a poem. I stole it from him on Saturday.'

'You stole it?'

'We were in his room. We were arguing when his wife called. I noticed the paper on his desk and took it when he wasn't looking.'

'Why?'

'Sometimes I just took things from him, alright? I just took them. A scrap of writing. A pen. An old theatre ticket. I told you it wasn't rational.'

'Would you read me what was on that paper?'

'Why does this matter so much?'

'Please, Delia.'

She pulled it out of the suitcase where she had tucked it. She unfolded the paper, and read:

> when the words dissolve
> we spill together, you and
> I, cloudburst of rain

'He wrote that?' I said.

'Yes. It's a haiku.'

'I didn't know he wrote haiku.'

'It started after the stroke. As I said, he could barely speak for the first few weeks. A rehab therapist at the hospital tried to work with him using routine language exercises, but they seemed to annoy Ken, as if he was bored—which is just like Ken. I mean, the man had suffered a stroke but didn't lose his aesthetic sense. So the therapist started trying out different kinds of text for the exercises, and haiku seemed to work best. The poems were short and vivid, holding Ken's interest. He developed an appreciation for the form after that, and began experimenting with his own writing once he'd left the hospital.'

'That's remarkable. He told you all this?'

'Yes, although he didn't like to show his work. He regarded himself as too much of an amateur. He let me see a few, though. I thought they were quite nice. A bit romantic. When I saw this one on his desk I couldn't resist taking it.'

I walked to the window and gazed toward the Pfannli.

'What's wrong?' she said.

'There's something else I need to tell you.'

She came beside me. 'What is it?'

I took the heart watch out of my pocket. 'This is yours, isn't it?'

'Yes,' she said, after a hesitation. 'He gave it to me.'

'When?'

'A couple of months ago, after he returned from a conference in Budapest. He got it from a gypsy. How did you know it was mine?'

'I spoke with the German woman. The mother of the girl that you gave it to. Why didn't you tell me it was yours when I asked you?'

'Where did you find it?'

'Over the waterfall. It was tangled in a bush on the cliff edge, overlooking the spot where he died. Why didn't you tell me, Delia?'

'I didn't put it up there. I didn't kill him, if that's what you're getting at. I just gave it to the girl, alright? I don't know what happened to it after that.'

'I believe you. But why didn't you tell me?'

'It took me off guard when you asked. I didn't know you, and I didn't trust you at that moment.'

'When did you give it to the girl?'

'Sunday morning. It was the day after Ken and I

argued. I was on the hotel porch and saw the girl playing with her doll. Her brother was pestering her. I don't speak any German, so I went over and braided the doll's hair. That seemed to make the girl happy. She noticed my necklace and I pulled it up, showed her the watch. She liked it and I gave it to her. We put it on the doll.'

'You gave it to her even though it was a gift from Sir Kenneth?'

'I felt sorry for her. I had a soft spot, I guess. I don't usually care about kids, but recently...you know...'

'I understand.'

'And Ken had asked me to stop wearing it. I'd hardly ever put it on anyway—I thought it was a little tacky. He also told me to delete all our emails and messages. Seems he wanted to get rid of any evidence that we were involved.' She held out her hand. 'May I see it?'

I gave her the watch.

'I forgot to reset the time for her,' she said, studying it. 'Why is the chain broken?'

'I don't know how that happened.'

'You found it on the cliff?'

'That's another mystery. The girl's brother—Klaus is his name—he took it. He ran off with it. That was on Sunday night. His mother eventually caught up to him but by then he'd hidden it. But not over the waterfall. I'd like to hold onto the watch for a while, if you don't mind. I promised to return it to the girl.'

She passed it back to me. 'Her name is Claudia.'

'Claudia and Klaus? That's original.'

'If the boy didn't put the watch on the cliff, then where did he?'

'I'd rather not say anything yet.'

'What, are you playing the inspector now?'

'I'm not playing the inspector. I just don't want to speculate and cause rumours.'

'You think somebody killed him?'

'I'm not sure. The police will probably want to look into it.'

'So you're going to tell them?'

'Yes. Tomorrow.'

'That doesn't exactly help my case, you realize? If you found the watch over the waterfall, then it stands to reason that I was up there and pushed him off the cliff. That's what they'll think.'

'But you didn't do it, right? And as far as we know, it was the boy who last had the watch, not you.'

'I don't like that you're hiding something from me.'

'I know, but it wouldn't be fair to start speculating without any solid evidence.'

'You're not a detective, Conner.'

'I didn't say I was.'

'Do you have any idea how hard this is for me? How can you be so insensitive? If somebody murdered Ken, then I want to know who. Maybe you don't know what it's like to care about somebody that much—'

I started for the door.

'Wait, I didn't mean it that way.' She came to me and took my hand. 'We don't have to talk about this. We can talk about anything. Just don't leave me alone. Please.'

I tugged my hand away. 'I'm sorry, Delia. But I have to go.'

'Why?'

'Because I need to talk to Flange.'

'You're going to talk to that pervert?'

'There's something I need to ask him. And then I need to rest. It's been a long day. I'll call you in the morning, okay?'

TWENTY

I WENT DOWN the corridor to Flange's door and knocked. There was no answer. I sent him a text message asking where he was, and a few seconds later, as I headed down the stairwell, his response buzzed on my phone: *Outside by the north wing.*

I went out and circled around the building and found him on a wooden bench amid some flowerbeds. He had changed his pants since the alp, but was still wearing the suit jacket. There were crusts of mud on the sleeves.

'What were you doing in her room?' I said.

'I was looking for her.'

'You could have knocked on her door instead of climbing over the balcony.'

'I did knock. Of course I knocked. But I was worried about her. I thought maybe something had happened to her.'

'And then you broke into her room?'

'I didn't *break* in. The balcony door was unlocked.'

'How did you get to it?'

'From the third floor. The room over hers is being renovated. The door was open.'

'You climbed down?'

'I let myself over. The railing is solid.'

'I can't believe you, Flange.'

'I didn't plan to go down there to get into her room. I just wanted to *see* if she was in there. What if she had killed herself or something? I was getting worried. She hadn't responded to any messages. When I realized the balcony door was unlocked, well—everything sort of unraveled from there.'

'Unraveled?'

'Are you involved with her, Conner?'

'No, of course not.'

'Don't lie to me.'

'How can I be involved with somebody I only met two days ago?'

'This isn't 1950. Two days is long enough to get married and divorced.'

'Am I detecting a hint of jealousy, Flange?'

An expression of hopelessness welled up in his eyes. 'I'm sort of in love with her.'

'In *love* with her?'

'And a little obsessed, I suppose.'

'Is that why you went through her suitcase?'

'I was just looking around and then—I couldn't help myself. You wouldn't know what it's like.'

'I wouldn't know? Why wouldn't I know?'

'Because you're so bloody controlled! So moral and upright! Oh yes, the classic God-fearing man! But you know what? You'll be sleeping with her soon enough. You'll see. You may be strong, Conner, but you're not that strong. Not as strong as she is. She seduced Ken and she'll seduce you. And the irony is, you don't even know how to have sex!'

'Flange.'

'It's true, isn't it?'

'What does it matter?'

'Answer the question! Have you *ever* had sex? Do you even masturbate?'

'This is irrelevant.'

'It's like you're stuck in the Middle Ages! Even monkeys masturbate, Conner. Even dogs rub against objects.'

'I wasn't created as a monkey or a dog. I was created as a man. I try to behave like one.'

'Meaning you have no real life experience. Zero.'

'Are you saying I need experience to figure out what monkeys and dogs already know?'

'You're missing the point. I mean you can't understand how to be in a relationship unless you're comfortable with the physical side of things.'

'Do you think sex is so complicated?'

'Intimacy is very complicated.'

'Intimacy and sex are not the same thing.'

'They're interwoven.'

'The hardest part of intimacy is getting to know a

woman's heart and mind. Not her breasts.'

'Don't you have any sexual impulse at all?'

'I have a great deal of it. But sex belongs in a certain place.'

'Stop right there. Don't even try to lecture me on marriage.'

'I wasn't going to. Did you take anything from her room?'

'No.'

'Because she'll notice if you took anything.'

'Well, I took these.' He opened the side pocket of his jacket, revealing a wad of crumpled fabric.

'For goodness' sake, Flange. Is that underwear?'

'They're socks.'

'You took her socks?'

'I have a slight foot fetish.'

'I can't believe you would go to such lengths to satisfy your appetite.'

'It's not about appetite. See, this is what you don't understand. When you fall in love—'

I waved away the word. 'You'll have to return those, you realize?'

'How am I supposed to return them?' He touched the side pocket protectively. 'And she might not notice.'

'Are you the one that hacked into her computer?'

'Her computer?'

'Somebody was spying on her. Somebody had access to her email and would have seen any messages between her and Ken. You're saying it wasn't you?'

'No! I would never have done that. I only knew they were meeting in his office. I hung around after hours to keep an eye on them. I suppose that counts as spying, but it's the old-fashioned kind of spying. I didn't break into her machine, and I certainly didn't spread that story around. I wouldn't do anything to hurt her. Does she think *I* did it?'

'Yes.'

'Oh God! Now I'm really finished!'

'Will you be quiet?' I said, glancing back. The pension stood nearby, across a patch of grass. It was a large three-story chalet with the wall of the cliff running behind it. Cows were grazing on the mountain slope beyond, barely visible in the fading light.

'So the story is true?' Flange said. 'He got her pregnant?'

'Yes, it's true.'

'Was it her idea or his—and who decided on the abortion?'

'I can't get into the details, Flange.'

'Did he force her to do it?'

'It's her private business.'

'But she told you? She shared all these intimate details with you?'

'Some of them.'

'She obviously feels something for you. She tells you about her affair, her secrets. It's a sign. She has feelings for you and you're not even an atheist—you're a Jesus freak who won't even have sex before marriage!'

'Get a hold of yourself. I need to ask you something. Did you know that Sir Kenneth wrote poetry?'

'Who told you that?'

'She mentioned it to me.'

'It started at the hospital. It was part of his speech rehab.'

'You've always known, then?'

'It wasn't a secret, but he didn't like to talk about it. He was private about it. I tried to respect him by not talking about it to others. Did he write poems for her too?'

'Please, Flange. Just relax.'

He sighed, wringing his hands.

'There's one more thing I wanted to ask,' I said. 'Do you remember Sunday night, after we came back to the hotel from our walk? You played billiards with Leo and Blakey.'

'What about it.'

'Where was your jacket?'

'My what?'

'Your jacket. We came in from the outside. Do you remember? It was raining. We encountered Leo as we arrived, and we walked into the hotel lobby together. I went to my room but you stayed with Leo. Where did you go next, and where did you put your jacket? Did you take it off?'

'Why does this matter?'

'It's just a question.'

'But there's something behind the question.'

'There is, but I'm not able to share it yet.'

'You're still trying to connect the dots, aren't you? I wish you would stop that!'

'Just tell me what you did with your jacket that night.'

He leaned back wearily. 'I went to the billiards area. Leo and I both did. I believe we took our jackets off then. They would have been wet. I think we threw them down somewhere. Maybe on the couch or the chairs.'

'The same jacket you're wearing now?'

'Yes. You saw me wearing it. Why?'

'What about Blakey? He must have arrived just after you did. Was he wearing a jacket as well?'

'He probably was. He'd been outside too—he mentioned the rain.'

'Do you remember a boy hiding behind the couch?'

'This is what you were asking Blakey about, isn't it?'

I nodded.

'Yes, I remember him. He ran up just a couple of minutes after you'd passed by with your cup of tea. He hid behind the couch and then his mother came and scolded him. He'd put a doll in the tree, the potted one. She took the doll down and then led the boy away.'

'When did the billiard's game end?'

'Blakey and I played until around ten. Leo left early.'

'Why?'

'How should I know? He seemed a bit gloomy that night, although that's not unusual for him.'

'And you all took your jackets with you?'

'I assume we did. Why are you asking this? Is this

about Ken? Or Delia?'

'I'll tell you soon. I promise.'

'Don't create any more scandal, whatever you do.'

'Speaking of scandal, I'd like you to give me those socks.'

'What?' he said, clutching the bulging side pocket.

'You can't keep them. Or do you want her coming after you? This could spell trouble for you, Flange. She might file charges with the police. I'm sure I could talk her out of it.'

He sighed. 'Alright.'

I slipped off the small pack I was wearing. Inside was a white plastic bag containing leftover bread and two pieces of Emmental cheese. I took the food out and opened the bag before him.

'Drop everything in here,' I said.

He pulled out the socks in a wad and deposited them, muttering to himself.

'And that was everything?'

'Yes. Two pairs of women's sports socks. Orange with white stripes. Mildly worn.'

'Good night, Flange.'

'She won't be worth it,' he said as I walked off. 'She'll break your heart! She might even break your God!'

TWENTY-ONE

I WENT BACK inside and headed to the billiards area. Nobody was playing, and I walked slowly around the table, thinking back to that night. I remembered passing the table on my way to the lobby and then walking back again with my tea a few minutes later. My only clear recollections were of Flange's affable face when he invited me to join in the game, and of Granger bent over the table about to take a shot, his eyes flashing up at me with an expression of contempt. Blakey was present but I could not place him. I had no recollection of the couch or the jackets.

The jackets: Flange wore the suit jacket, and Blakey, I recalled, had a blue fleece. I could not recall Granger's.

I took out my phone and scrolled to the photos I'd taken earlier on the alp.

A grey windbreaker.

I looked at the couch. At least one jacket must have been draped over it, and maybe all three. I walked behind it and squatted down, as I had earlier today, and tried to imagine I was the boy. He had to have slipped the watch into the jacket pocket without disturbing the jacket itself—without causing it to slip off the leather backrest. It might be easier with Blakey's fleece or Flange's suit jacket, whose fabrics were heavier than Granger's windbreaker. But the boy probably wasn't thinking about that. He would have simply gone for the nearest pocket, whosever it was.

'May I help you?' came a voice.

I looked up. It was the hotel manager, his head tilted with mild perplexity.

'I lost something,' I said.

'What did you lose?'

'A memory. Excuse me.'

I got up and continued down the corridor. I went through the double doors and a line of pot lights flashed on, triggered by motion detectors. I passed Granger's room, and Flange's, and halted before Blakey's.

I knocked. A few seconds later the door opened. 'Oh hello,' Blakey said.

'I didn't mean to disturb you. I had a question. That night you were playing billiards with Leo and Flange, were you wearing a jacket?'

He grinned, a glob of chocolate clinging to the edge of his tooth. 'You're quite curious about that night, aren't you?'

'I am.'

'I was wearing a jacket when I arrived, but I'm pretty

sure I took it off. I'd just come in from the rain.'

'Do you remember where you put it?'

'I must have hung it somewhere. It's not the kind of thing I keep track of.'

'What about the couch? Is it possible you draped it there?'

'I don't remember.'

'What about Leo's and Jeremy's jackets? Were their jackets on the couch?'

'Really, I don't recall.'

'There are also two chairs by the window. Might you have–?'

'Look, I'm tired and need some sleep. I don't remember anything about jackets.'

'Of course. Good night.'

He closed the door. I walked back up the corridor and rapped on Granger's door a few times. There was no answer and I was frankly relieved. I doubted he would have taken kindly to my questions.

I went back to my room. The curtains were open and darkness was falling, dimming the mountains to a shadowy mass. I suddenly realized how hungry I was; I hadn't eaten since lunch. I'd told Delia I would call her in the morning, but I wondered now if she might be up for a late night meal.

Was she still awake?

I slipped off my pack and checked my phone. There were no messages.

I opened up her number and pecked out a text: *Are*

you still up? Do you want to go for a late supper in the village?

No, I thought. What am I doing?

I remembered the verse on the wall of the church: *How can a young man keep his way pure? By guarding it according to Your word.*

Dammit, why did God always get in the way?

I tapped the *send* button. The message flew off with a *whoosh.*

There was nothing wrong in seeing her. I would return the socks. I would offer an apology on Flange's behalf. We would stroll back to the village for a meal. We would talk.

Just talk.

I paced the room, clutching the phone, waiting for her reply.

Where was she?

I went out to the balcony and looked up toward her room. Light was streaming out.

Should I call out?

No. Too desperate.

I settled into the balcony chair. My feet were humming from the day's hiking. Stars were becoming visible over the dark ridge of the mountains. I heard a sound, a grunt, and then a figure leaped over the balcony next door. It was Zach Blakey. He glanced over his shoulder, but didn't notice me slumped in the chair, and went hurrying through the meadow.

I got up and watched. He was heading down toward

the road, his podgy figure waddling quickly, and soon he vanished behind a chalet. I leaped over my balcony railing and jogged after him through the grass.

He'd said he was tired. He needed to get some sleep.

Lies.

My phone buzzed.

I pulled it out of my pocket and looked. *Sure. Can we leave through the lower lobby? I don't want to be seen.*

I ran between the chalets and saw Blakey on the road. He was heading into the village. I stopped and tapped out a reply to Delia: *Wait in your room. I need a few minutes.*

I started after him again. I was about twenty or thirty metres behind, keeping close to parked cars and bushes. He slowed to a walk but his pace was brisk. The hotel patios were busy and people were wandering leisurely up and down the main road.

He turned at the village church and started up the slope. I lost him as he circled around the gondola station and then caught up again on the other side, in a residential neighbourhood. I saw Margaret's chalet where Flange and I had visited yesterday. I recognized the chime with the streamers over the door.

For a few moments Blakey seemed headed for it; then he followed a path between the chalet and another home and vanished. I ran down the path and spotted him in the middle of a road. He had stopped and was looking back and forth.

I crouched behind a hedge. We were at the upper edge of the village. There were only a few chalets across the road. Behind them was the dark upward sweep of a mountain slope.

A phone glowed against Blakey's ear. He began speaking and a moment later a man's voice called out from somewhere. Blakey turned, and I spotted a figure waving from an open doorway at the end of the road.

The voice called out again: 'Hallo, Zachary!'

'Guten Abend!' Blakey replied with a laugh.

He jogged down the road to the chalet. He shook hands with the figure. They went inside and the door closed.

I stared at the house. My phone buzzed: *Still coming?*

I wrote back: *I need a few more minutes.*

Ok, she replied. *I'm waiting.*

I walked down the road to the chalet. It had a tiny front lawn, and several figures were visible through the thin curtains of the lower windows.

I moved closer and made out three young men. They were on the floor in front of a large screen where race cars were speeding down a seaside road, engines blaring. Two of the guys were jiggling consoles in their laps and a third was on a couch watching the game.

Where was Blakey? Why was he here?

I lingered a couple of minutes, puzzled and suspicious, and a bit guilty too, knowing it probably wasn't my business. I was about to leave when the Preacher came into the room. He'd cleaned up since the alp, his hair smooth and dry, his expression calm. The young men looked up at him as he spoke, and then one of the guys aimed a remote at the screen. A volume bar appeared and shrunk. The Preacher retreated down a hallway and the video game continued, quieter now.

I walked around to the side of the chalet. I caught the sound of voices from somewhere, and a faint laugh, but saw nothing. The neighbouring residence was dark. After a little waiting, I moved along the timber wall, passing a doorway and a cement patio. The meadow beyond climbed up and lost itself in the shadows of the wooded slope.

Peering around the back corner of the chalet, I noticed an open window. I moved closer, trampling over a soft flowerbed, and peered inside. Blakey and the Preacher were seated before a computer screen. They were watching a video. The light in the video was dim and there was no sound, but you could not mistake the two people or what they were doing. Delia was leaning over Sir Kenneth, her hair swaying back and forth across her shoulders as she rocked her body over his.

I stared, so astonished that I almost failed to notice the buzzing of my phone.

It was her. *Everything ok?*

I looked through the window. The Preacher turned to Blakey and spoke; the video froze and disappeared. Blakey moved his hand over a mouse and a photograph appeared on the screen. Then there was another. He began scrolling through them. Flashes of her naked body.

I heard something again and turned. Two figures were wandering out of the dark meadow.

‘Was machen Sie hier?’ one of them called out. ‘Wer sind Sie?’

I ran.

They came after me shouting. I went down the side of the chalet and caught my foot on the edge of the patio, stumbling a few steps, and then righted myself and ran on toward the road.

They were still pursuing me. The air was cool and smelled of grass and barns, and the mountains hung like dark drapes around the valley. Somehow I recalled a scene from childhood, of playing in the street with the other boys and the voice of my father calling me home. And I was running, running with reckless speed, all the way up to the door of our house, hoping I might impress him.

God, I hated the bastard.

I cut through the path beside Margaret’s garden and one of the guys caught me from behind. I tumbled to the ground and something struck my head. Everything went black.

TWENTY-TWO

My next memory was of music. A piano concerto. A room of dark timber beams and the smell of wood. A wholesome smell.

A painting hung above me. The Anker painting of a fair-skinned girl peeling potatoes. She looked familiar, as if I'd known her all my life.

'You're finally awake,' said a voice.

I was lying on a couch. There was a pillow under my head. I turned slowly and beheld a woman sitting in a chair a few feet away.

'Do you remember anything?' Eleanor said.

I was slow to register the words. My head was throbbing. She rose from the chair and approached. Her mouth was framed in wrinkles and her eyes looked tired.

'You're in Margaret's house,' she said. 'You got into a scuffle last night. Do you remember? What were you doing out there?'

The memories came back to me. I felt a wave of

dizziness as I tried to lift my head. Eleanor took my arm and helped me sit up. I looked about the room and noticed an upright piano. Nobody was playing it. The concerto was coming out of a stereo on a shelf, where a vinyl record was turning, although in mild confusion I could not help looking at the piano, as if it ought to be coming from there.

'Did you know them?' she said.

'Who?'

'Those boys from last night.'

'No. I didn't know them.'

'Why were they after you?'

I was about to speak but hesitated. I knew I could not answer her. She didn't press the matter and continued: 'They ran off as soon as we came out. You don't expect such things in a village like this. Apparently there have been scuffles because of the conference. Are you hungry? Do you want me to call someone?'

I felt around my pockets.

'Are you missing something?'

'I had a phone.'

'I didn't notice a phone with you.'

'I must have dropped it.

'Do you remember us helping you in? You were conscious for a while.'

'I remember running.'

'You were a little woozy but you were talking. You said you needed to rest. You fell asleep.'

'Here?'

'Yes. You were on the couch all night.'

'Well, well!' came a cheerful voice. Margaret clomped into the room in rubber boots and gardening gloves. 'He's alive, is he? Good! The morning bread won't go to waste!'

'I was just telling him what happened,' Eleanor said. 'I'm sorry, I don't recall your name.'

'Conner.'

'I was telling Conner about last night.'

'How are you feeling, young man?' Margaret said.

'Alright. Just a headache.'

'We decided not to call the ambulance. I should say *I* decided—I hope you don't mind? You wouldn't be any more comfortable in the hospital, and probably less so, and God knows what you might pick up in there. I say it's best to avoid hospitals until it's too late. I worked as a nurse in Manchester for six years, I ought to know.'

'Margaret sat with you for most of the night,' Eleanor said. 'Do you remember her waking you?'

'Vaguely. It's a bit blurry.'

'She woke you a few times, to make sure you were alright.'

I gave Margaret a nod. 'Thank you.'

'It's nothing. We wouldn't want you falling into a coma, would we? Ha-ha, I'm only teasing. Now let me take a look at you.' She sat down on the coffee table beside the couch and took off her gloves. She held my wrist and watched my face. She said my pulse was fine and my pupils looked okay. She asked me the date and my name and where we were. I had no trouble answering.

'Good as gold,' she said. 'Your breakfast is on the table if you want it. If you feel like vomiting please use the bathroom—it's by the back door. Don't exert yourself any further today or tomorrow. Now I must be getting back to my garden. There was a sprinkle of rain in the night and the slugs are out.'

She clomped off. Eleanor took my arm and helped me up. I was able to walk to the kitchen on my own. The table was set with bread, jars of marmalade and honey, a pot of tea, and packets of cheese. Margaret was visible through the back door, bent over the garden, picking at the earth.

Eleanor set a clean saucer and cup before me. 'I need to make a phone call,' I said.

'There's a phone right behind you.' She indicated an old-fashioned box on the wall beside the light switch.

I got up and took the receiver. I couldn't remember Delia's number.

'Is everything alright?' Eleanor said.

I put the phone on the hook; it wouldn't have been a good idea to call Delia from here anyway. 'I should get back to the hotel,' I said. 'What time is it?'

'Half past eight. You should eat something first. Then I can drive you.'

I spread some butter and jam on a slice if bread. Eleanor poured cups of tea.

'I'm sorry to impose like this,' I said.

She gave a forced, fleeting smile. 'I have experienced a

number of impositions over the past few days. I can assure you that you are the least of them.'

Her thin eyebrows were like a pair of unhappy scales tipped toward the bridge of her nose. I chewed my bread in silence, pitying her, fearing that more impositions were coming. The video. The photos.

'I knew about Kenneth's involvement with that girl,' she said as if reading my mind. 'I knew it before I read it in the news yesterday. Unfortunately, nobody seems to consider the fact that my husband was no longer the same man when he got involved with her. You won't read about *that* in the news.'

'You mean he had changed?'

'Yes. The stroke altered him. Most people assume that he'd recovered, but it's not true. He wasn't the same Kenneth. His personality was altered.' Her hand was trembling and the teacup clattered as she placed it onto the saucer. 'I wish people could understand that. They judge him, but it's *she* who ought to be judged. She was in her right mind, not him.'

I nodded. 'It's well known that a stroke can affect a person's behaviour.'

'You are a doctor?'

'No. But I've studied a bit about it. I'm doing a PhD in psychology.'

'At Mount Albert?'

'Waterloo, actually. Sir Kenneth gave a guest lecture there early last year. It was a full house, I recall.'

She took a breath, knitting her fingers together.

Green veins snaked over the backs of her bony hands.

'I'm very sorry,' I said.

'He lost his faith,' she said quietly.

'What?'

'In atheism. He was going to tell everybody at the conference. He had discovered...' She shook her head. 'It's absurd. He had discovered...'

'Discovered what?'

'It was a spiritual feeling. Or so he called it. You might have found out, had he lived a day longer. It doesn't matter now. You can tell Jeremy and Leo Granger and all the rest of them. Let them be shocked. It doesn't matter. His reputation is already in shambles.'

'What do you mean by *spiritual feeling*?'

'No doubt it was a hallucination. A result of some kind of damage to his brain. There were times when he would stare into space, like a man lost in a vision. The doctors had wondered if he was having seizures, but that wasn't how Kenneth experienced it. He said it was something profound, something greater than himself. He felt it inside of him and around him like a conscious energy. What nonsense. I told him so. His mind was playing tricks.'

'And this went on until he died?'

'It faded over time, but it never went away. He would get glimmers of it. Echoes of heaven, he called it. Ridiculous! He meditated in an effort to recover it. He wrote poetry to express it. He even prayed—can you imagine that? Sir Kenneth Chatwin on his knees? I told him to be rational. He had been such a rational man until then. I asked him to get help, but he refused. Then he got involved with that girl. *That*, if you ask me, was the real proof of what had become of him. He'd lost his mind utterly.'

'Did he tell anybody else about this?'

'Maybe he told *her*? I don't know. I know he struggled with the feeling. At times he resisted it. It went against everything he believed in. But the thing about a feeling, you see, is that it can persuade a person of anything if it persists long enough. A solid feeling is more convincing than a solid argument. And that is what overcame my husband. A feeling! Of all things! It changed him completely in the end, and he couldn't keep it a secret anymore. A few days before we left for Switzerland he decided, with great reluctance, that he would reveal it at the conference. It was time to be honest with everyone, he said. He even wondered if it might be an opportunity to promote a better dialogue between atheists and non-atheists. But that was just a faint hope. He knew the likely consequences. He would be mocked and laughed at. People would think him mad. Everything he ever worked for, everything he had built up, would crumble. But you see, it's crumbling anyway.'

TWENTY-THREE

NOW I UNDERSTOOD the extent of her pain. She had almost lost her husband to the stroke, only to discover that she had lost him in another more fundamental sense. The change was more devastating than death because it fractured their relationship and undid his life's work—something that death could never have accomplished.

I wondered if I should tell her about the video from last night. It might prepare her for what was coming.

Or maybe I could stop it? Assuming it wasn't too late.

'I should return to the hotel,' I said.

'Yes, of course. Forgive me for going on. I can drive you.'

'I am sorry for what you have gone through, Ms Chatwin.'

She nodded. 'I was going to tell all this to Jeremy and Leo. You are free to mention it. I won't keep the secret anymore.'

'If I may ask, did your husband leave any writing or

notes behind? He was supposed to give the opening talk at the conference.'

'I never saw anything. The last thing I saw him writing was his poetry. Leo has those pages.'

'Is that what he took from you yesterday, after you collected Sir Kenneth's belongings?'

'Yes. Although I doubt Leo will have much use for them. I doubt anyone will. The poems aren't much good, I'm afraid. They'll become another source of mockery. I'm sorry, I don't mean to ramble on like this.'

We rose from the table. We went down the hallway and I slipped into my hiking shoes. She opened the door. The woman from the BBC and a man with a recorder were standing outside.

'We just had a few questions, Ms Chatwin,' the woman said.

'Are you aware of the video of your husband and Ms Stoltz?' the man said.

Eleanor pushed the door shut. She bolted it. 'Oh God, what are they talking about? What video?' She leaned back against the wall, breathing rapidly. 'What are they talking about?'

'There is a video of your husband and Delia Stoltz. There are pictures.'

'Oh God.'

'Let me help you,' I said, touching her arm.

'You cannot help me!' she shouted. 'Leave me alone, leave me alone!' She crumpled to the floor, pressing her face in her hands.

The back door opened. Margaret came hurrying through the kitchen. 'What is all this shouting? What is going on, Eleanor?'

'There are reporters outside,' I said.

'What on earth for?'

'It's more news about Sir Kenneth and his student.'

Margaret opened the door. 'Get away, both of you! Get off my property or I shall call the police!'

I hurried out, slipping between the two reporters. They called out to me but I kept running. It was a cool day and high clouds were drifting in from the south end of the valley, skirting the jagged snowy peaks, while lower clouds were coming up from the north end in thick shreds, brushing over the wooded slopes. The road led me past the gondola station, but rather than continuing down to the main road I veered onto a paved lane and followed it between the chalets. It was a short cut to the hotel—the one I had discovered two days ago.

The lane turned into the dirt path; it ran up the shelf of rock and along the cliff and within a few minutes I was approaching the Pfannli. The Hotel Iselin appeared over the treetops. My head was throbbing and I hurried onward, jogging over the stream that fed the clattering waterfall.

As I reached the top of the cliff steps, I heard the crying of an infant. I halted and peered down toward the meadow. I saw the Frenchwoman. The child was bundled against her chest in the sling. The woman reached the trees and turned, and walked back the other way, passing right under me.

The infant's cry welled up between the hotel and the cliff. I backed away from the steps and listened. The cry was hollow and distressing and something occurred to me.

Instead of going down the steps, I continued along the cliff edge. It was a slender ridge of rock with trees on one side and the precipice on the other. The hotel was just below me, and as I reached the other side of the building I saw the bench where I'd found Flange yesterday evening after he fled from Delia's room. Beyond was the pension and then a cluster of trees.

I pushed on, my head pounding. The trees below began to thin and at the same time the cliff tilted downward, the smooth grey rock falling toward a muddy gap. It was a few metres wide and spilled into a larger field of mud. The rock rose up again on the other side of the gap and continued along the lower slope of the mountain.

The earth above the gap was trodden with hoof prints. The smell of manure emanated from the ground, and the gentle clinking of bells drifted down through the mist. I realized there was a cow pasture on the slope above—the pasture I'd seen yesterday evening while speaking with Flange.

I clambered down to the gap. There was no way around the mud field. I stepped into it and my foot immediately sunk to the ankle. There was a squelching sound as I pulled it out. My shoe almost came off. I trudged twenty or thirty paces through the mud, my feet squelching with each step, before reaching the grass.

I stamped off some of the mud and then began running again, down across the meadow and around the trees. Flecks of rain had begun to fall and through the mist I saw people setting up a large tent beside the hill across from the hotel. I was dizzy and paused at the porch steps, gripping the railing, and then staggered on toward the main doors.

The hotel lobby was packed. People were standing around and talking and looking at tablets and newspapers. It was after nine o'clock and the day's conference sessions should have started. I saw a headline on a laptop: *Atheist and Lover Caught on Camera.*

I moved through the crowd, looking about. Blakey was chatting with one of the Oxford volunteers. The Ovaries woman. I went to him and grabbed him by the sleeve.

'Hey, what are you doing?' he said.

I pulled him to the wall. 'You leaked the video,' I whispered.

'What are you talking about?'

'I know it was you. You broke into her computer. You found out about the affair and leaked it to the media. You leaked everything. I saw you with the Preacher last night. I saw the video you were showing to him. Your friends almost beat me up.'

'That was *you*?'

'Yes.'

'God. I am sorry.'

'How could you do this, Blakey? Do you realize what you've done?'

He glanced over his shoulder. He moved closer. 'Please understand.'

'Did you kill him?'

'No! I just put out the video.'

'And the news story from yesterday?'

'Yes, but that was all. I didn't kill him. I had nothing to do with his death.'

'Do you have any idea of the pain you've caused?'

He stared at me, gnawing fretfully on his mouth. 'I was called to do it,' he said suddenly, his eyes welling up. 'You need to understand.'

'Who called you?'

'What do you mean, who? The Lord.'

'You're using God to justify what you did?'

'God saved me. I was a hateful drunk until he came into my life. He saved me. He changed me, and...'

'And what? Gave you a mission?'

'There's a reason why I ended up at Mount Albert. Don't you see?'

'You've destroyed people's lives.'

'Me? They destroyed their own lives! All I did was shine a light on what was going on.'

'You swear you didn't kill him?'

'I told you, I had nothing to do with his death. The accident—falling off the cliff—that was obviously God's punishment. Anybody can see that.'

'How did you find out about the affair?'

'I hacked into his computer and looked around.'

'And then you broke into her machine as well? Is that where you found the sex video?'

He nodded. 'It wasn't the only one. There were others.'

'I don't want to hear it! You realize you'll be held accountable for this?'

'And who's being held accountable for the murder of the baby in Delia's womb? Aren't you a Christian? We are here to fight against sin.'

'I have enough sin in my own life, Blakey. It's more than I can handle.'

'Please, I'm asking you not to tell anyone.'

'Where is Delia?'

'In her room, talking to the police. Please don't tell anyone. We're on the same side. We follow the same God, don't we?'

Flange walked up. 'There you are, Conner. I didn't see you at breakfast. What happened to you? You look awful. What happened to your shoes?'

'I was outside,' I said, looking down at my feet. They were still caked in mud.

'You must have heard about the video?'

'Yes.'

'Another bloody disaster.'

'Why is everybody out here? Why aren't they in session?'

'The police are questioning Delia. Word got around

and people are waiting to see what happens next. It's nonsense! She wouldn't have killed him. Nobody killed him. As for that video, I hope they find the people behind it and fry them alive. Hell is too good for them.'

'I'm sure the truth will come out. What do you think, Blakey?'

'Well, I—'

'Conner,' Flange said. 'May I speak with you in private? Would you excuse us, Blakey?'

Blakey nodded and slipped away.

'About yesterday,' Flange said. 'I was out of line. I said things to you that were mean and insulting. There was no excuse for it and I wanted to offer my deepest apology. If you can find some way to forgive me, I would be grateful.'

'You're forgiven, Flange. There's no harm done.'

'We're still friends, then?'

I noticed Granger by the windows, sitting with some colleagues.

'Conner?'

'Yes, we're friends.'

'By the way, did you return those socks to her?'

'Not yet.'

'Because, you see, I was thinking it over, and it occurred to me that Delia has bigger problems at the moment than missing socks. Why upset her any further? They're only socks. You know, your shoes do stink, Conner. Where were you?'

I looked at my shoes again.

'You might want to change them,' he said. 'Do you have another pair?'

'Another pair,' I murmured, staring.

I looked at Flange's shoes. Brown loafers. They were fairly clean, except for some discoloration around the toes. Blakey had been wearing the vintage basketball sneakers, the ones with the black-and-white design. I couldn't recall anything unusual about them.

After a moment's thought, I went quickly to the memorial display and found the two pictures I'd noticed on the first day of the conference. One was of Sir Kenneth on the porch, writing on hotel stationery; Blakey and Flange stood nearby over the giant chess pieces.

Blakey was wearing the basketball sneakers—they were clearly visible. Flange's shoes were harder to see.

'What are you doing?' Flange said over my shoulder.

'Do you know when this picture was taken?'

'Saturday, just after lunch. I asked one of the staff to take it with my phone. It was a few hours after we arrived.'

'What about this one?' I said, indicating the photo of Sir Kenneth and Leo in front of the coffee machine.

'It was a bit later on the same day. I took that one.'

'Do you still have the pictures on your phone?'

'Yes, why?'

'Show me the one with you and Blakey. I want a closer look.'

Sighing, he took out his phone and found the picture. 'There.'

I took the phone from him and brushed the screen, zooming in on Flange's shoes. They were the same brown loafers he was wearing now, the same ones he'd been wearing for days.

'Conner? What's going on?'

I gave him the phone. 'Wait here.'

I made my way across the lobby toward Granger. He was at a table by the windows and I came to within a few paces of him, observing until he glanced at me. Then I walked back to Flange and pulled the photo of Sir Kenneth and Granger off the display.

'Excuse me!' the Ovaries woman said. 'That is *not* appropriate!'

'It's alright,' Flange said. 'We'll bring it back. What the hell are you doing?' he whispered, following me.

'Give me your phone again.'

'Why?'

'Just give it to me and I'll explain.'

I led him into the corridor and down to the billiards table, where I stopped and searched the Internet on his phone. I found the video of the debate on the alp. I played it, watching for the right moment, and then paused the video. Granger's shoes were visible at the bottom of the screen. My heart began racing.

'Conner?'

'Be quiet. I'm thinking.'

'About what? Will you please explain what this is all about?'

I looked at him. 'You might not like it.'

'Don't tell me it's another shock?'

'I'm afraid it is. But if you want to hear it then you need to listen to everything I'm going to say.'

'Of course I'll listen.'

I showed him the frozen image on the phone. 'Look at Leo's shoes,' I said.

'What about them?'

'No stripes.'

'So what?'

I showed him the printed photo of Sir Kenneth and Granger. 'Do you see Leo's shoes here? Look at them. They have reflector stripes. That was before Sir Kenneth died. But as you can see in the video, Granger was wearing different hiking shoes, shoes without stripes, the day after he died. He's still wearing the same hiking shoes today.'

'I'm not following you.'

'Let me back up. Do you remember this?' I asked, digging the heart watch out of my pocket. 'I know that you denied ever seeing it. But you probably knew that it was Delia's.'

'Alright, you got me. I did notice her wearing it once.'

'And you didn't tell me because you were trying to protect her. You didn't want any suspicions to fall on her—in case Ken really *was* murdered.'

'Who ever said he was murdered?'

'Just listen.'

'It was an accident, Conner! I didn't admit knowing the thing was hers because I didn't want you to think I had my eye on her.'

'Granted. But allow me to finish. You said you'd listen.'

'Fine, I'm listening.'

'What you probably don't know is that Delia gave the watch to a little girl staying at the hotel. I spoke to the girl's family yesterday. She's with the German family. Her brother is the kid with the loose tooth. He took the watch from his sister on Sunday night, the night before Sir Kenneth died. It was hanging around her doll's neck before he pulled it off. He confessed to hiding it in a jacket right here.' I patted the back of the couch.

'While we were playing pool?'

'Yes. There were three jackets, one belonging to each of you—and at least one of them was draped over this backrest. The boy, as you recall, was crouching behind it, right where I'm standing. He slipped the watch into one of the jacket pockets to hide it from his mother. It happened to be Leo's jacket, but of course the boy didn't know that. The choice must have been random. When the billiards game ended, Leo took his jacket back to his room, not realizing that the watch was in the pocket. The next morning, Sir Kenneth left the hotel at a quarter to six. You told me that yourself, correct?'

'Yes. The staff mentioned it.'

'He went outside for his morning walk. He climbed up to the cliff. And Leo was with him.'

'Nobody mentioned seeing Leo.'

'Because Leo didn't go out through the main doors.

As Sir Kenneth circled around the hotel and crossed the meadow toward the cliff, Leo spotted him through his balcony window. Sir Kenneth would have passed right by it. Leo grabbed his jacket, put on his shoes, and hopped over the balcony. He caught up to Sir Kenneth and they climbed to the clifftop together. You see, there was something that Leo needed to talk to him about. It was something urgent, something that Sir Kenneth had confided in him recently—maybe as recently as a day or two before. Sir Kenneth was planning to announce it at the conference. In fact, he probably intended to reveal it to you and the rest of the group at the meeting on Monday morning. The meeting he failed to show up for.'

'What was it?'

'That he had lost his faith in atheism.'

'*Lost his faith?*'

'I know it sounds absurd, but Eleanor will confirm it. I spoke with her this morning. The stroke altered something in Sir Kenneth, gave him access to a new experience, some kind of spiritual feeling that changed his perspective on life. He was going to announce it at the conference. Leo, knowing this, was opposed to it—and you know how strong Leo's views are. He must have been furious. It was going to destroy everything they had worked for until then. They must have argued. And then, deliberately or in a fit of rage, Leo pushed him off the cliff.'

'That's outrageous! Leo, a killer?'

'Hear me out, Flange. He pushed him, and Sir

Kenneth grabbed Leo's jacket before falling, snagging the watch from the pocket, snapping the chain in the process. But the watch must have slipped out of his fingers as he went over the edge. It got tangled in the bush below the precipice—and remained there until I found it later that day. Leo didn't know anything about the watch, of course. All he knew was that his friend was dead. It was quite foggy around that time, as you yourself told me, and Leo probably couldn't see the body, but there could be no question of Sir Kenneth's fate given the height of the cliff and his age and frailty. Leo would have been panicked at this point—and he must have decided not to tell anyone. Meaning it would look like an accident. A slip. A fall. But he had to get back to the hotel before he was spotted. The fog had given him cover up to then, but now a new problem emerged: he heard crying in the meadow below. The crying of an infant. The same cry you heard that morning around six o'clock. Are you following all this?'

'Go on,' he said coolly.

'The mother of the infant is a Frenchwoman from the pension next door. She often walks the baby around the meadow below the cliff. I've seen her. She was out there a few minutes ago. That morning, as Leo pondered his escape, he realized that he couldn't go down the steps. Someone was there and he might be seen despite the fog—a fact which could later connect him to the crime. His choices, now, were limited. He could stand there and wait for whoever was walking the baby to go away, but it was dawn and becoming lighter and the fog might lift.

The longer he waited the more likely it was that somebody else might come outside and see him. A second option would be to follow the path toward the village and then to head down to the main road and circle back toward the hotel. But that is a very roundabout route, and would carry an even greater risk of being seen.'

People were passing in the corridor. I fell quiet for a moment and studied the expression on Flange's face. A narrowed eye. A look of doubt, of cynicism.

I went on quietly: 'A third option, the option he ended up taking, was to follow the path in the other direction along the cliff, in the hope that there might be another way down. And there is. The path continues onward a short way and then descends into a mud field at the foot of the mountain. It had rained earlier that night and the mud would have been quite thick. It still is today. That's what you see on my shoes. Mud and cow manure. I was there a few minutes ago. Leo's hiking shoes would have been as bad as mine when he reached the hotel. He would have circled around the building from the other side—going around the porch and over his balcony.'

'Without anyone seeing him? Without the mother noticing a man climbing over the railing?'

'His room is furthest from the cliff. He could have gotten in without the woman seeing him, especially with the fog. As for anyone else, who else was there? The hotel was almost empty. It was us, two elderly couples, and the Germans.'

'And you're trying to tell me that he had to change his

shoes afterward?'

'Exactly. It would have been useless to wash them. They would still be damp and mud-stained when the police arrived, as he surely knew they would in a few hours. He wore sandals that morning when he came to the waterfall—do you recall? He pushed away a slug with his sandal. That afternoon he drove into Frutigen to pick up Eleanor at the police station. Frutigen has many shops. He could have easily stopped in one of them to buy a new pair of shoes before going on to the police station. I'm sure all this can be confirmed through merchant records.'

TWENTY-FOUR

FLANGE BETRAYED A skeptical smile. 'You've been very creative with the facts. I'll give you that much.'

'You're saying you don't believe me?'

'His death was an accident, Conner.'

'I've just laid everything out for you. Don't you see how it all fits together?'

'What I heard was a good story. But just because a story is good doesn't mean it's true.'

'Then how do you explain the watch? The boy said he put it in a jacket.'

'Maybe he was lying. Maybe he threw it somewhere before he reached the billiards area and somebody else dropped it off the cliff.'

'What about the shoes? How do you explain them?'

'I don't know. Maybe he has two pairs of shoes.'

'Why would somebody bring two pairs of hiking shoes on a trip to Switzerland?'

'Who knows? I brought two toothbrushes.'

'It all fits together, Flange—the watch, the jacket, the mud, the shoes.'

'You see, this is your problem. You're stuck on the idea that everything has to fit together in some profoundly meaningful way. That's probably why you believe in God.'

'God has nothing to do with this!'

'You see patterns in things, Conner, you see designs, and you can't resist them. But some things don't have a deeper meaning—like a second pair of shoes or a second toothbrush. Sometimes things just *are*, for quite trivial reasons. You have to stop connecting the dots. Okay? Once and for all. Now can I have my phone back?'

'I prayed for a sign the night before Sir Kenneth died.'

'What?'

'I had doubts about God's existence. I asked him for a sign that he was real. And the next morning Sir Kenneth was dead.'

'You see, this is what I'm talking about! It's all just coincidence! Do you really think God is behind this?'

'Actually, I don't. But somebody is.'

I started toward the south wing.

'Where are you going now?'

'I'm going to talk to the police.'

'Are you crazy? Conner! And that's my phone!'

'It's evidence now.'

I ran through the double doors and dashed up the stairwell to Delia's room. A plain-clothes officer answered at my knocking. Inspector Black Dove and

Delia were seated at a table.

She hurried to the door. 'What happened to you?' she said. 'I couldn't find you last night.' Her eyes were reddened from crying.

'I'm sorry,' I said, taking her hand. Then I called to Black Dove: 'I know who leaked the video. And I know why Sir Kenneth died.'

The Inspector ruffled his brow at this bold declaration, but he allowed me in and listened patiently to the story. I told them about Blakey as well; I actually started with Blakey, which had the effect of making Black Dove take me more seriously when I got to the matter of Sir Kenneth's murder. Delia listened with dismay, and more than once she wiped her eyes, stifling tears.

When I'd finished answering their questions the police took Flange's phone from me, along with the photo of Sir Kenneth and Granger, and then headed downstairs to Blakey's room. He went quietly with them, meek as a lamb, but Granger was another matter. He was still in the lobby and started bellowing when they explained he had to come to the police station. He guessed I had something to do with it and shouted furiously at the sight of me. They had to put the cuffs on him.

Everybody came out to the porch and stood at the railing as Granger and Blakey were led into the back of the police car. The assembly of worshippers across the road, who had launched into hymn singing, became quiet when they saw what was happening. They started coming out from the tent and gathered at the roadside, watching through the soft rain.

Blakey gazed despondently through the rear window. The vehicle pulled out of the parking lot and drove off. Turning, I noticed Flange staring hard at me. I couldn't think of what to say to him and went back into the hotel.

I'd given Delia the key to my room, knowing that the reporters might start knocking at her door. I found her sitting at the window with her suitcase. Her eyes were tired and swollen.

'It's over,' I said. 'They're gone.'

'Did they get the other guy? The Preacher?'

'The Inspector contacted the village police. They're going to pick him up.'

I sat down beside her. I put my arm around her, and she turned toward me and we held each other.

'I thought you didn't want to see me last night,' she whispered. 'I thought you were playing some kind of game.'

'I don't play those kinds of games.'

She pressed her face against mine. Her tears were warm on my cheeks.

'I feel like I can trust you,' she said.

'Of course you can.'

There was a knock at the door. I got up and looked through the peephole. It was the woman from the BBC, her eager eyeball staring back at me.

I retreated quietly to Delia. 'Reporter,' I whispered.

'They just won't leave me alone.'

'Let's get out of here. Now.'

'Are you serious?'

'We can take the next bus to town.'

'But you need some rest, Conner.'

'I can rest on the bus.'

'And they'll see us leave if we try to get out.'

I glanced toward the balcony. 'We can go out that way.'

'Over the balcony?'

'Why not?'

She opened the balcony door and went out. She peered about and came back inside. 'It's clear, for the moment.'

'Then you should go. I can meet you at the bus station in a few minutes. I still need to pack. And I need to speak to Flange.'

'Why?'

'He's upset. He didn't want me to go to the police. He's having difficulty accepting what Leo did.'

'What about what Jeremy did to *me*? Did the pervert say anything about *that*?'

'He did, actually. He's quite sorry.'

'Oh really?'

'He said he went into your room to see if you were okay. He was worried about you.'

'And then he decided to sniff my underwear?'

'Well, he—'

'I don't want to talk about it. It's disgusting. Makes me sick.'

I nodded. 'I understand.'

'Anyway, I should get going while the coast is clear.'

I offered to take her suitcase but it was small and she insisted she could manage. She hopped over the railing and I passed over the suitcase and a small black carrier that held her laptop. 'Just don't keep me waiting this time,' she said, slinging on the carrier.

I stared at it, wondering about the other sex videos that Blakey had mentioned. Was this a thing she often did with Sir Kenneth—or with all her lovers?

'What's wrong?' she said.

'Nothing. I'll be forty-five minutes. An hour tops.'

'Don't push your luck this time,' she smiled.

She took my hand and pulled me closer and gave me a peck on the cheek. Then she turned and hurried down through the meadow, lugging the suitcase at her side. As she reached the foot of the clearing she looked back and waved. I waved and she disappeared between the chalets.

I went into the bathroom and took a painkiller and brushed my teeth. I changed my clothes and gathered up my things and overturned my backpack, emptying the contents.

The little plastic bag of socks fell out and spilled open. Orange socks with white stripes. I took one and unfolded it. The bottom was slightly soiled, with a bulge where her heel had pressed. The front of the sock was angled a little, suggesting the outline of her naked toes.

A surge of desire billowed up in me. I wanted her. It was foolish, I knew it, but I wanted her—whatever might come of it. It didn't matter if it worked out or not. I just wanted to be free for once and follow my feelings without filtering everything through God.

Anyhow, it wasn't as if I was behaving like my father. I wasn't betraying a wife, a family. I wasn't betraying anybody—except God himself. God and his moral law. *Watch and pray that you may not enter into temptation.* But the moral law seemed like old-fashioned finger-wagging, and God seemed so absent that it was hard to take him seriously.

'You may as well not exist,' I muttered, taking the other socks from the bag.

The heart watch was inside. I stared at it, confused. I had given the watch to Inspector Black Dove.

I reached into the bag and took the watch by the chain and held it up. It was the same watch. The chain was broken. I put it to my ear and it was ticking.

But I *did* give him the watch. I was sure of it—unless my throbbing brain was failing me? I stared at the thing, the silver heart, dangling before my eyes. Then I noticed it wasn't six hours behind. In fact, it was local time. Almost eleven o'clock.

I looked at the orange socks. They had been in Flange's jacket pocket. He had pulled them out in a wad. Had dropped them into the plastic bag.

What have I done? I thought.

I had Black Dove's card in my wallet and tried his number, but couldn't reach him; I left a message. I thought of calling Delia but I still couldn't remember her number. I slipped into my muddy shoes and hopped over the balcony railing and crossed the meadow to the cliff. I climbed up the steps to the top, keeping a firm grip on the rope railing, and hurried toward the village. Tatters of dull cloud drifted overhead. A wave of dizziness hit me at the gondola station and I leaned against a wall until it passed and then continued up the road. I hammered on Margaret's door.

Eleanor opened it. 'You're back,' she said. 'What is it?' She looked at my shoes. 'What's wrong, what happened?'

I held out the heart watch. 'You had one just like this. Didn't you?'

'Where did you get that?'

'It belongs to Delia Stoltz. Your husband bought it for her during the trip to Budapest. He bought it from a gypsy. I know you were on that trip—your sister mentioned it. Did Sir Kenneth get one for you too?'

'No,' she said after a silence. 'But...'

'But what?'

'That's Delia's?'

'Yes. Your husband gave it to her, but she gave it away to a girl at the hotel a few days ago. It was still set to eastern time then. Someone must have reset it to local time soon afterward—probably the girl's parents. But there's another watch just like this one, a watch that I found on the edge of the cliff, right at the spot where your husband died. *That* watch was still six hours behind. Whoever brought it to Switzerland didn't reset it.'

'And where is it? Do you have it?'

'I gave it to the police. Was it yours, Ms Chatwin? Were you with Sir Kenneth that morning?'

'I can explain everything. Please. But not out here.'

She opened the door and stood back and I entered. She closed the door and asked me to wait. She walked down the hall to the kitchen and I leaned against the wall, catching my breath and struggling with another dizzy spell.

I heard the sound of clattering. To my left was the sitting room where I'd slept all night, under the painting of the girl peeling potatoes.

I looked toward the kitchen. 'Ms Chatwin?'

I started down the hall and she came into view. She was rummaging through a closet.

'Ms Chatwin?'

She turned at me with a rifle. It was an old-fashioned sort, with a long shaft and a broad wooden end. She pulled back a metal bolt and held the barrel inches from my chest. 'Don't think I can't use it,' she said. 'This was my father's. He taught us how to shoot.'

I raised my hands. 'Please, don't.'

'It's a rather strange coincidence,' she went on, her voice tremulous. 'An unfortunate coincidence. But then, he was a good seller, that old gypsy. He caught your eye from a distance and smiled and kept waving until you came over. There were many heart watches on his table. He assured me they all brought good luck. "All of them?" I said. "Yes," he said, "they're all special. All magical." There was something quaint about it. I have a weakness for trinkets. So I bought the watch, the good-luck watch, and I managed to misplace it that very day. I didn't see it again until weeks later, after I was back home. It was at the bottom of my travel kit. I remember the mild shock on Kenneth's face when he saw me wearing it—and I didn't understand why at the time, but I see now. He had bought the same one for her. From the same gypsy. I suppose that's a bit of *bad* luck, isn't it? I suppose I ought to find that gypsy and tell him he got it all wrong.'

'You put the watch on that morning.'

'I wanted to feel better,' she whispered bitterly. 'But makeup and a necklace can't turn back the clock of age. Can't make your cheating husband fall in love with you again.'

'That's why you went to the cliff. That's why you pushed him. He pulled the watch off your neck and that's why you returned later. To find it.'

'Shut up! He deserved what he got after going to bed with that slut! Impregnating her! Making a mockery of our marriage! No, I am not to blame. I am not to blame at all.' She took the collar of her blouse with her free hand and yanked it, tearing it. She gripped the rifle and shook it at me. 'I will tell them you came back here. You tried to rape me. There was a struggle and I found Margaret's gun. They will believe me. You belong to a vile generation, you young people. Selfish and vile!'

'But I've already called the Inspector, Ms Chatwin. I left him a message about the second watch. I said it was probably yours. If you shoot me, he'll know why.'

There was a click behind me. I glanced back and saw the front door open. It was Margaret, grinning with a cloth bag in her hand. I looked at Eleanor.

'What is going on?' Margaret said.

'Vile!' Eleanor cried, shaking the barrel at me.

The rifle gave a blast and knocked her backwards. Margaret screamed and I found myself on the floor, ears ringing, sulphur burning in my nostrils.

My first thought was that I was dead. My second was that I hadn't forgiven my father—and it was too late.

I heard the clatter of the rifle as Eleanor threw it aside. She ran down the hallway. I pushed myself up a little, my head reeling, and looked at my chest and arms, searching for blood. I noticed a jagged hole in the timber wall. Margaret was sitting on the floor with a hand on her gaping mouth.

I was weak and dizzy. I lay down again, my cheek pressed against the cold floor, and stared at the painting of the girl.

TWENTY-FIVE

THE TRUTH IS seldom what we expect, although our expectations pave the way for it, like a path through darkness and shadows.

The police found Eleanor's rental car near the top of a mountain. It was parked at the end of a muddy track beside a wooden hut. It appeared, from what they could surmise, that she had continued up the slope on foot, through the trees and around the old avalanche barriers, until she reached the summit. She must have wandered for some time through the ankle-deep grass and gorgeous wildflowers. She must have caught the occasional ring of cowbells through the breeze. Somewhere along the way she slipped, or hurled herself, into a ravine. She was found dead the next morning in a pile of boulders. Her skull was shattered.

I never had a chance to speak with Leo Granger again, but I'm sure he never forgave me for my mistake. As it turns out, he'd purchased his new shoes the night before Sir Kenneth died. Granger was in the village after supper when he noticed a hole in his hiking shoes. He picked up a new pair at a sports shop and was actually wearing them when he returned to the hotel, although nobody noticed during the billiards game. As for the sandals that he wore on the morning of Sir Kenneth's death, that was just chance. He had a pair of sandals and happened to put them on that day. The sandals, like the shoes, were another dot in a series of dots that I'd wrongly connected.

The conference was dealt its final blow that day. The Oxford volunteers took down the memorial display, boxed up the books and pictures, and plodded off to the bus station. A number of guests lingered to the end of the week, trying to get the most out of the money they'd paid, but it rained and the mood was gloomy. Here and there about the hotel I caught snippets of discussion about the state of Sir Kenneth's mind during the last months of his life. Most people agreed that he was the unfortunate victim of a damaged brain. Despite that, his poetry, as everyone knows, was later collected and published to near-universal praise (expressing, in the words of one critic, 'a potent blend of sacred and erotic force').

As for Delia, she had waited for me at the bus station for over two hours, until the reporters found her. I don't blame her for taking the next bus out. It was the second time I'd jilted her. I managed to contact her by phone after she returned to Mount Albert, and she was entirely understanding when I explained what had happened. At this point, however, whatever had drawn us together, whatever energy had pulsed between us, dissolved with barely a sigh. We wished each other an amicable farewell. I never saw her again, although years later I noticed her name with a MD beside it, listed on a research paper in pediatric medicine.

There were efforts to charge Blakey and the Preacher for their part in the scandal, but nothing ever came of it. Blakey dropped out of graduate school and entered the seminary. He went on to become the pastor of a church somewhere out west. Flange did a postdoc in the US and then landed a job back at Mount Albert, where he remains until this day, teaching and doing psychology research. We are still good friends, and he still enjoys warning me against my tendency to 'connect the dots'.

As for me, I remained at the hotel for three weeks after Sir Kenneth's death, with free lodging courtesy of the hotel manager, who regarded me as a sort of hero. I never did return the heart watch to the Munich girl, and I would not have wanted to, given its tragic associations. However, she was more than pleased to accept the gift of a small purse, embroidered with a kitten, which I found in one of the village boutiques. (I did not forget her brother: he got a dinky car.)

The peacefulness of the valley and the imperious calm of the mountains did me much good. My head stopped throbbing and my spirit revived—revived remarkably, probably because I knew I shouldn't be alive. When that rifle fired, I felt the kiss of death brush against me; I felt the trapdoor of hell drop open under my feet. If I were Jeremy Flange, I might have given thanks to chance that I was still here—and even more alive now, without the weight of the old bitterness that I'd held against my father. But I was not Flange, and there was only one I could thank: the Father I did not fully comprehend, yet now trusted in a deeper way.

Last but not least, I plucked up the courage to talk to the milk maid. She bore some resemblance, I realized, to the painting of the girl peeling potatoes. Her name was Annika, and it turned out she was doing a Master's degree in classical Greek and Latin. The hotel was just a summer job.

We went to the village bakery on our first date. We had a beautiful conversation over lattes and sweet almond croissants, and watched the Wimbledon final on the overhead screen. The Swiss favourite lost the championship match by a whisker, although I hardly noticed at all.

AFTERWORD

I have had the pleasure of visiting Switzerland many times, and most of the settings in *Death of an Atheist* were inspired by actual locations. The 'village' in the story could easily describe any number of villages and small towns in the Swiss mountains. The grassy alp on the 'Alpkäppli' (where the debate takes place) was modelled on the Engstligenalp, a lush plateau in the Bernese Oberland with a waterfall that tumbles 600 metres to the valley below. The little 'Pfannli' waterfall near the 'Hotel Iselin' is my own invention. Any similarity between the 'Iselin' and other hotels and establishments in Switzerland is purely coincidental.

The cover image for this novel is from Arnold Böcklin's Self-Portrait with Death as a Fiddler. Böcklin was a Swiss symbolist painter from the 1800s. I am not an art expert, but the juxtaposition of a living man beside a skeleton captures one of the underlying themes of the novel: What does death mean?

It is a question we must all answer sooner or later, and our answer will largely define our worldview.

PGH

www.ingramcontent.com/pod-product-compliance
Lightning Source LLC
Chambersburg PA
CBHW061229170626
46809CB00007B/2572
9781988604114